W0010189

The DoomsDay Prepper

By

Eileen Curtright

JournalStone
San Francisco

JOURNALSTONE
YOUR LINK TO ARTISTIC TALENT

Copyright © 2015 by Eileen Curtright

All rights reserved. No part of this book may be used or reproduced by any means, graphic, electronic, or mechanical, including photocopying, recording, taping or by any information storage retrieval system without the written permission of the publisher except in the case of brief quotations embodied in critical articles and reviews.

This is a work of fiction. All of the characters, names, incidents, organizations, and dialogue in this novel are either the products of the author's imagination or are used fictitiously.

JournalStone books may be ordered through booksellers or by contacting:

JournalStone
www.journalstone.com

The views expressed in this work are solely those of the authors and do not necessarily reflect the views of the publisher, and the publisher hereby disclaims any responsibility for them.

ISBN: 978-1-942712-30-5   (sc)
ISBN: 978-1-942712-31-2   (ebook)
ISBN: 978-1-942712-33-6   (hc – limited edition)

Library of Congress Control Number: 2015938645

Printed in the United States of America
JournalStone rev. date: June 12, 2015

Cover Design: Cover Art & Design: Chuck Killorin

Edited by: Aaron J. French

The DoomsDay Prepper

I

I'd seen it coming for a long time, but mostly I kept it to myself. You don't become branch sales leader by popping off about the End of Days, the coming social, political, and environmental collapse. *Imminent collapse.* And when your field is insurance, well... you better believe I held my peace.

At Alamo Mutual, I was trading in lies. I'd pull up a chair at some stranger's kitchen table, accept a glass of orange juice I didn't want, and explain how a given policy would mean lifetime security and protection. The clients were awkward and prone to nervous laughter, like people unused to discussing their own deaths and the catastrophic loss of all they owned. I wanted to hurl the orange juice against the wall and scream about bodies in the streets and days of darkness and rivers of fire, like a methed-up street preacher, but instead we'd shake hands and I'd promise that with a whole-life policy they could sleep easy. "Peace of mind" was the phrase our regional head was pushing in those days. So I'd get the signatures and take the forms back to my office. I had wood paneling and a philodendron in there, and the radio turned down low. I'd sharpen a pencil and get back to it, assessing the risk that such and such building would burn or flood, or this or that business would fail during the term of the policy, as if things would go on in this comfortable way for the foreseeable.

It didn't feel right. "I'm a fraud," I said to myself. I was standing at the front door of Jeff Robert and Marissa Beal, holding a briefcase, sweating in my suit and tie. If I'd had a shred of honor, I would have gone back to my car and left these people in peace. But when Marissa came to the door I put on a smile and stuck out my hand. "Oh, but we're family!" she said and pulled me in for a hug. I prayed the back of my shirt wasn't sweaty, but I knew by her recoil that it was.

"Thanks so much for seeing me," I said, assuming a slightly cringing manner. That's the way you do it—deferential at first, uncertain of your welcome, but inside a quarter of an hour the dynamics would shift. In the end, they'd sign where I told them and pass over the check.

I followed her into the house, evaluating her claim of kinship. Where we family, really? Marissa is my wife's second cousin, but if I'd seen her since our wedding, I couldn't now recall it. Anyway, it had been long enough that my weight gain was clearly a shock to her, but she did a passable job of hiding it. Marissa led me into the kitchen where Jeff Robert was flipping grilled cheese sandwiches on the griddle. He hugged me, too, with the spatula still in hand, and I decided second cousin by marriage didn't count.

"I'm interrupting," I said, even though this was the time of our scheduled appointment.

They both denied it and then offered me a grilled cheese sandwich which I accepted, along with a glass of orange juice. I find people grow uncomfortable when a fat man eats, but I pretended not to observe the mixture of concern and disgust on their faces as I folded my sandwich on top of itself and dispatched it in four large bites. Then I drank the orange juice without coming up for air.

"Let me ask you this. If something—God forbid—if something were to happen to you tomorrow, Marissa, would Jeff Robert and your boy be provided for?"

"We have our savings," Marissa said.

I began to lay out some numbers. It's important to dance lightly over all the death and maiming, chronic illness and catastrophe that might torpedo the average suburban life. I took them quickly to another image—Jeff Robert and the boy, Louis, happy and secure, their futures certain, because of the wise and responsible decisions that were made at this kitchen table today. Marissa teared up. It moved her, this image. Never mind that if it came to pass, it would mean she was in the ground and Jeff Robert was dating again.

"Peace of mind," I said, tapping the pile of papers. And then I signed them for an enormous life policy, far more than any reasonable estimate of Marissa's future earnings would suggest was necessary. There was a time when I would not have stooped to such a thing.

They thanked me repeatedly as they walked me to the door, their arms draped around each other. I didn't linger. Insurance is like an aphrodisiac for some couples. It's almost like renewing your vows.

As I walked to my car, I was filled with disgust. I'd been an insurance man once, but now I was just working a con.

* * *

I rode the elevator back to the office with Trip Edmonds, our regional head, swabbing my forehead with a handkerchief. Trip also wore a full suit in 98 degree temperatures, but he never sweated out of context; only on the elliptical trainer had I ever seen his shirt damp. He could see by my tie that I'd been out on a call.

"Did you score?"

"So close," I said, crossing my fingers. There was no reason to lie to Trip, other than that his grin annoyed me, and that my conscience was tender on the subject of this check. I couldn't face Trip's whoop of congratulations, the obligatory high-fives. I'd rather let him think I'd struck out.

"You'll reel them in," he said, kneading my shoulder. He's a hands-on manager. But I could tell he was pleased I'd failed. Trip thought I was gunning for him. I *had* been gunning for him, once, before the signs became conclusive. Now I put in my hours, but weekends I devoted to the plan—holidays too. Sick days? You better believe it. I wrapped myself in an electric blanket and read up on how to purify water, how to improvise a splint from common objects. But no matter how much I learned or how much I prepped, I could see that it was not enough.

"Back at it," I said as the doors opened to the seventh floor.

* * *

"I feel like a fraud," I said over blooming onions that night at Señor Queso's. The Alamo Preppers Group met every Tuesday in the party room in back. There were twelve of us at the table, passing the onions and a platter of potato skins, and I'd had one too many beers. "I'm out there hawking policies that'll never pay out. My customers may as well light their premiums on fire."

"There's an idea," Hank said. He lived just half a block from my house. Insurance was his livelihood, too, but instead of bringing us together, our common profession made us uneasy with each other.

"Well I feel guilty," I said. "Don't you feel guilty, Hank?"

He chewed a piece of onion and didn't say a word.

"The information is out there for anyone to find," Cerise said. She and Hank prepped together. Prepping is ideally a family activity, but my own wife, Lisa, had never made an appearance at an event or social. "Who *are* you?" Lisa said once, when she found me at my workbench, dipping arrows into neurotoxic poison and sipping a cup of cold black coffee. Now I found it easier to keep my activities private.

"You can't help those that won't be helped," Hank said.

Lisa was firmly in the camp of those that won't be helped. Officially, I was no longer involved with the Alamo Preppers, because she deemed it—my "hobby"—to be borderline deranged. As I sat there eating fried onion, my wife was under the impression that I was at my Tuesday night exercise group, sweating in sync with a trainer and trying to shed the extra pounds. It was a necessary deception, one she'd forgive when I was able to keep her and our girls alive.

"All I'm saying, Eric, is it's fine to sit here and talk about your feelings, but when the day comes it's kill or be killed, my friend." Hank threw a scrap of fajita to his dog, Cormac, who lounged at his feet.

Cerise nodded. "I can and will shoot to protect my family and property *right now*. And when the E.O.D. hits, all bets are off."

"Well I sure won't cross *you* in the last days, Cerise," Milo said. Then he winked at me.

"Oh, I might go easy on you. You're just a kid," Cerise said. She reached across the table and stroked his beard. I took a fried jalapeño from the communal platter.

"Kid or not, each and every other person represents competition for scarce resources. No mercy. That's got to be the policy if you want to survive. Of course, not everyone will have the stomach for it." Hank looked at my gut, which was now protruding over the waistband of my athletic shorts. "The weak will be winnowed out early on."

Hank ordered another round. He was drinking more than usual and behaving with more swagger than he had before. But we were all changing. The ground shook so often and spewed fire so frequently that even some civilians began to express concern that a calamity of some type might be in the works.

People stocked up on foodstuffs at Costco and wrote their congressmen about fracking, but we preppers were far beyond that. Milo had a boat stocked with protein bars and a de-salinator parked in the lot of his apartment complex.

There were other, more ambiguous signs that even here, among friends, we were unwilling to discuss.

"I'll tell you what keeps me up at night," Hank said.

"The ghosts?" Milo said. "There was one in the tree by my window last night, playing a corrido." It was as if he'd told an off-color joke or disrespected the right to bear arms. Even Cerise recoiled. But Milo doesn't always pick up on social cues. He chewed on in the appalled silence, oblivious.

"What keeps *me* up at night is that Rodney compound," Hank said. "They got guns. Shelter. They certainly got the numbers." Bat Rodney and his extended family had been prepping for decades, preparing to take on the New World Order with a loose militia of paranoid rednecks. They wanted no part of Alamo Preppers, and in fact, words had been exchanged between members of their group and ours at a recent trade show. "They'll be sitting pretty," Hank added.

"Oh, I wouldn't worry," Milo said. He winked at me a second time. Milo had become fixated on sea levels recently, and by that wink he meant to convey that the Rodneys would be at the bottom of the ocean with the rest of us.

"The prudent thing would be to make a move now. But it's risky. You'd have to time it just right," Hank said.

"What kind of a move?" I said.

"Jesus, Eric. A *move*. The irony is, it's easier to pull it off before the rule of law collapses, when nobody's really expecting it."

"So what are you going to do?"

"What do you mean? I'm just saying, it would be the smart thing."

"You mean the smart thing would be to go and kill all the Rodneys now, before they kill us later."

Hank held up his hands. "Hell, I know it sounds bad. But these are the tough calls a commander has to make."

"A commander?" I said. Hank blushed. He'd already awarded himself a post-apocalyptic rank. Commander Hank. The nerve of this guy. "So are you going to do it, then?"

"Are you going to do it then?" Hank mocked, adopting a sing-song voice. "Look, Eric, it's not that simple."

"Why not, Commander?" Hank talked tough, but I was beginning to suspect that talk was all it was. His military buzz cut, his camo pants—certainly he wrapped himself in signs of manly swagger and preparedness, but even Milo's plans made more sense to me, and *Milo* wore a waxed mustache. Hank's operating theory of the end had been randomly culled from message boards—a bit of federal government overreach, a dash of the Book of Revelation, a strain of supervirus manufactured by French Canadian separatists.

At the other end of the table, Lorna and Doug, our president and first gentleman, clinked their spoons against their glasses. "If I can have your attention one minute," Lorna said, rising from her chair. "A toast is in order. Hank—share your news."

Whenever a prepper makes a significant step on the road to preparedness, they announce it to the group. I was toasted when I secured a field toilet and six weeks of MREs. That was over a year ago.

Hank took his time. He subjected us to a long windup in which he thanked Lorna and all his fellow preppers for their constant support. It wasn't just *his* achievement—it was a testament to the strength of this group. I stared at the remains of the cooling onion, hating him.

"Stand up, Cerise, this is your moment, too." He took her hand. He went on a while longer about how truly blessed he was before he spit it out. "We bought a Don Cheevers," Hank yelled, raising his arms in the touchdown sign. I bit the tines of my fork till I heard my teeth grind against them. The whole table burst into applause and Hank kissed his wife on the lips.

I was just sober enough to remember to clap, which I did, exactly three times. Three big wet claps of my clammy drunk's hands, damp with beer glass condensation. More than that I could not do. A Don Cheevers—the leading name in disaster preparedness luxury in the south-central-Texas region. Don Cheevers hollowed out missile silos and bomb shelters and remade them into high-end condominiums that could see a family of four through any number of disaster scenarios in comfort and style.

Hank looked so smug, like he just might ascend to heaven trailing clouds of glory. "Concrete walls four feet thick," he said. People were shaking his hand. He'd pick us off one by one through the specially designed sniper holes if we even *approached the perimeter* of his Don Cheevers on Day Zero. Couldn't they see that? But they were just happy for their fellow prepper whereas I, God help me, I wanted to put my teeth to the man's throat.

"Cheer up, buddy," Milo said, slapping my back. He leaned in to me and whispered. "That Don Cheevers will be nothing but a watery grave." He laughed behind his beard without making any noise. Milo is one of our younger members, still under 30, and he makes his living baking artisan bread. His theory of the end is that the waters of a bloated, poisonous Gulf will drown the Alamo City and environs. It was true that a Don Cheevers would be of no use in such a scenario; I only wished I had his confidence that that's where we were headed.

"Go buy yourself a second-hand canoe or some water wings and you're way ahead of this asshole," Milo whispered. I found it far more likely that death would come from the ground beneath our feet, but I nodded rather than raise objections. If Lorna overheard she would drop the hammer on the both of us. Talk prep all you want, but the bylaws of the group prohibit discussing the cause of D-day with any specificity. This keeps our meetings from devolving into arguments over solar flares vs. reversals of the earth's magnetic poles or what have you. Anyway, I appreciated the sentiment. "Thanks, Milo," I said.

"What's the joke?" Hank said. He eased back into his seat and gave me a look that suggested the joke was me. I invest in maintaining my personal appearance—my profession demands it. My hair is cut in a salon that serves herbal infusions; I buff my shoes with lambskin. If my mouth was now stuffed with sour cream and potato, this did not reflect my preferences. The weight gain was a deliberate strategy; everyone knew that. And yet right now, I just looked the pig.

"My love life," Milo said, grinning. His dating troubles are an ongoing source of amusement to us all. It's hard to date outside the prep community, and even harder to date within it.

"Poor baby," Cerise said, tracing her fingers up his arm.

"Now where you at with the water purification system, Eric?" Hank said.

"Lisa said no." To obscure my intentions, I'd pretended the system was for a family vacation I was planning: a rustic, multi-day campout deep in the wilderness of Big Bend country. Lisa had shot down both the purchase and the trip. *I'd rather die.* Her exact words.

"Oh boy. She'll really be kicking herself when the time comes," Cerise said. "How are y'all planning to manage without potable water?"

"Maybe I'll just cut her loose," I said. It was sarcasm. I love my wife, but I was in a dark place.

"You do that, I might take her on as a concubine," Hank said.

"Please," I said. "Cerise—come on—don't let him talk like that."

"I'll talk however the goddamn hell I want," Hank said.

"Not about my *wife*. Man, come on."

"Not cool, Hank," Milo said.

"We'll have a duty to repopulate the earth," Cerise said. "Many men will take on concubines. It's not a sexual thing."

Hank raised his eyebrows to suggest that it might not exactly be a non-sexual thing either.

"I don't think that kind of talk is good for group cohesion. We've got to be able to trust one another, Hank." I was groveling, because I knew he could do it—make my wife his concubine. He had the weaponry, the Don Cheevers, and he was pursuing a muscle strategy—he was fit and toned as a Hollywood actor. Lisa had once said he was "handsome as hell."

"I trust you about as far as I can throw you," Hank said. "Last bit's yours, Estrada," he said, pushing the plate toward me. I scooped up the unidentifiable fried bits that littered the plate and shoved them into my mouth; they tasted like nothing but grease. Soon enough, though, people would be wrestling their own children for scraps far worse than these.

* * *

I left the restaurant too buzzed to drive and walked the streets of San Antonio for an hour, thinking about Hank and his Don Cheevers. We were supposed to be a colony; that was the whole point. The Alamo Preppers had promised to have each other's backs, but now the Schoenfeld family would kick up their heels in that luxury bunker and let the rest of us fry, and nobody had even had the courage to call them on it.

Hank was a bastard now, but come the fateful day, he had the potential to be a true monster. I could picture him sitting bare chested on a throne wearing multiple necklaces and drinking wine from the skull of an enemy. "Well, that's Hank for you," people would say, because it would not be the least bit out of character. And they'd say the same thing about me, when they passed my severed head on a pike.

I wandered through tables of tourists drinking margaritas at patio restaurants, past wandering mariachis. The mood in the streets was festive. The the groundsmoke, the occasional bursts of lava that spewed out of city manholes, and the quakes—all these things were natural occurrences and now, without D.C. breathing down our necks, we would be able to respond to them with more efficiency and less waste. Nobody knew what was up with the birds; we laughed that off.

This world looked so solid, but it was about to be ripped away like a bandage. At last I found myself at the Alamo. It was all aglow, sitting like a big sleeping camel over its graves. Usually I feel nothing at all when I look at it, but tonight it struck me as a monument to un-preparedness, to men who hadn't had any strategy at all beyond drawing lines in the sand and sending grandiose letters. Well, they'd paid the price. As my family would, when the day came.

"Step aside, friend," a man in a coon skin cap and fringed chaps said as I stood in the plaza. He looked to be in some distress.

"What's the matter?" I said, failing to notice at first that I was speaking to a dead man. We'd made eye contact and now I was stuck. The safest thing was to bide my time. There was a theory that the underworld itself had been disturbed and was slowly leaking its inhabitants up to the surface. The industry maintained these incidents were caused by a naturally occurring and harmless hallucinogen found in the groundsmoke. Myself, I had no opinion.

"I'm late for the battle," the ghost said. His horse wandered over, clicking its hoofs against the cobblestones. Its mane was braided with flowers, but a flap of skin hung from its muzzle and its eye was an empty socket.

"The battle of the Alamo?" I said. The ghost looked at me as if he didn't think much of my intelligence. "You're way late. That battle's over."

"Who won?"

"The Mexicans," I said.

"Which side was I on?"

"By the look of your rags—meaning no offense—I'd say you were a Texian."

"Well, shit," the ghost said. "Goddamn it. I hate to lose." The breeze picked up and he just sort of blew away in the smoke.

"So do I," I said to the empty air. But it occurred to me then that *my* ancestor had not died here at the cradle of Texas liberty, as Hank's had. He'd *lived*. Under the command of General Antonio de Padua María Severino López de Santa Anna y Pérez deLebrón, the Mexican army had been better trained, better provisioned, and possessed of a far better plan. They'd fought to keep what was theirs, and they hadn't left a Texian alive.

* * *

The next day, I dropped by Hank's office just before the lunch hour. His place was a boutique agency, with his own name on the door. It was next to a gun shop, and inside a coffee-stained yellow carpet ran wall-to-wall. He had two silk palms in there and a murky fish tank. A single catfish swam back and forth above some plastic reeds.

At first glance, I found it hard to believe Hank was doing the kind of volume that could finance a Don Cheevers. My clientele would never set foot in a place like this, and that realization only made me angrier.

I cleared my throat, because the door's entry chime had not gotten the receptionist's attention. She was wearing a paisley tie and her gray hair flipped upward at the ends. She was reading a home décor magazine. "Yes?" she said, without looking up.

"I don't have an appointment," I said. "I'm a friend."

She raised her head and studied me. "A friend?" She said it as if the idea of Hank having a friend had never occurred to her. "Well then go on in. Knock first," she recommended when I had my hand on the door knob.

"Enter!" Hank yelled from behind the door. "Hey buddy. You get home okay last night?"

"Yeah," I said. "Look, about the Don Cheevers—"

"Would you like to see it?"

This was easier than I'd expected. "I sure would," I admitted. The general public was not given access to any Cheevers facility. Stop by for a tour? Forget it. First you had to be recommended by a current owner, then you had to pass a rigorous screening process, including a credit check, which meant I had no hope of even peeking inside one on my paycheck. How the hell Hank had cleared these hurdles I couldn't comprehend.

"I just bet you would," Hank said.

"I *said* I would." I assumed he was messing with me, offering a treat and then withdrawing it, a game a certain type of person likes to play with a child or a domesticated animal, but to my surprise he scooped up his keys. "Then let's go."

* * *

The Cheevers was near the city center, on the site of an Air Force base that had been decommissioned some years ago. A massive underground bomb shelter had been converted into 60 luxury condos, each more than 2,000 square feet in size.

I rode shotgun, beneath a seatbelt specially modified to accommodate Cormac, Hank's Irish Setter. Stray pieces of harness brushed against my suit, covering me with dog hair, as Hank talked up the Cheevers. These things had chef's kitchens with stainless fixtures and granite counter tops. Whirlpool tubs. The latest and greatest in alternative power sources, water filtration, and an on-site hospital and rec room. Future residents were already meeting up for barbecues and holiday parties. It was a "truly select group" of area movers and shakers. There was a rumor that Don Cheevers himself would be setting up camp here when the time came, and there was no greater endorsement than that.

Hank dropped names and shared details on the way over, and by the time I stepped out of his car, he'd made sure that I understood he would be spending his doomsday in more style than I had ever experienced. Hank implied that apart from the financial concern, there was no question of someone like myself being admitted here. I indulged in a little silent fuming as I brushed Cormac's hair off my sleeves.

* * *

The inside of the place was straight out of *Dwell*, but for the absence of natural light and one strange feature. Toward the back of the condo I found a floor-to-ceiling wire structure. It was separated from the main living quarters by a narrow hall. Hank had rattled off the features of every other amenity like a damn brochure, but on this wire room he was silent.

"I'm going to shoot straight, Eric. I don't make enough money to fund this place, you know that. I doubt my sales are 2/3 of your yearlies. So go on, ask me how I got it."

"How'd you get it, Hank?" I said, expecting to hear *wouldn't you like to know*, but Hank was unusually agreeable this afternoon.

"Premiums."

"I don't follow."

"My customers pay premiums on policies they'll never collect. You're an insurance man; I don't have to tell you the entire industry will collapse within the first twelve hours of an E.O.D. situation. My customers are simply throwing their money away."

"Mine too," I said. He wasn't wrong. The very thought of how little use even my best, most comprehensive products would be at the E.O.D.—that's end of days, in the parlance—robbed me of my peace.

"What was it you said the other night—might as well light them on fire? I couldn't agree more. So instead of incinerating those wasted sums, I redirect them here."

"You're stealing them."

"Only in a manner of speaking. Those policies are about to be useless. So Cerise and I prayed on it, and we've been given to understand, it's better that cash do some good for *someone*."

"But what if—I mean, Hank—" I was stammering. Hank stood there, waiting for me to say the words. *What if the apocalypse never happens?* Then he'd go running back to the group with the news that I was just a hobbyist. Now and then, lonely misfits mistook our society for a mere social club, a group weird enough to be accepting of those with below-average interpersonal skills. They usually slipped up and revealed that what they truly wanted was love and friendship, not a workable survival strategy for doomsday. We considered these types to be beneath contempt.

"Now hear me out," I said, holding up my hands before he got any wild ideas about my commitment level. "This thing is happening and soon. But in the meanwhile, all it takes is one historic flood. Or a 32-year-old drops dead of a heart attack. What then, Hank?"

Hank was a big guy with a cropped military haircut and pale, wide eyes. He didn't look the least bit brainy. He looked like the avatar of a video game, the type that would run repeatedly into a wall if you left the controller in position while you stepped out of the room to refill your Dr. Pepper. If even a small scale disaster befell one of his customers before the main E.O.D. event, he'd be left holding the bag, but he didn't seem to get that.

"Well, shoot, Eric, I guess that's where my comprehensive personal liability policy kicks in." The dumb bastard had thought of everything.

"So what do you want from me?" I was enough of a business man to see that a proposition was shimmering in the air between us and Hank was about to put it to me.

"I'm a little short," Hank said. "They won't give me the key to this thing till I'm paid in full. And I don't have to tell you, we're running out of time. You have contacts, Eric. All I need is a name." Hank's clientele was generally worth more dead than alive, whereas mine took out policies on their jewelry and recreational vehicles. "Get me in the door and I'll take care of the rest. You'll get your finder's fee, of course."

I pulled my collar away from my thickened, sweaty neck. I was suppressing a terrible rage. If anything is sacred in this soon-to-be destroyed world, it's the trust between agent and client. That trust must be rooted in plain dealing and forthright speech. That Hank believed I might be willing to betray one of my clients so utterly was an insult of the most dire kind. But I played along.

"I like your style, Hank. Let me think on it."

"Don't think too long," Hank said. The veins in his neck stick out when he grins. It's repellant. I looked away from him toward the wire enclosure.

"What's with the cage, Hank?"

Hank looked at me with pity, like I'd pronounced the *t* in escargot. "That's the pantry. Open air pantries—it's a modernist thing. They're just popping up in Texas but on the West Coast people swear by them. Better visibility, reduced moisture equals less food waste. That's going to be important in the early stages, before we get the community's hydroponic farm up and running."

"Huh," I said, noting a very serious-looking lock on the pantry's door. "Well it's a pretty long way from the kitchen, though."

Hank shrugged.

"And there aren't any shelves. Seems like maybe Don Cheevers cut a few corners after all. I don't know that I'd feel comfortable trusting my family to the design of a man who didn't think to put shelves in a pantry." I chuckled.

The vein in Hank's neck throbbed. "It's a *live* food pantry. No need of shelves. We'll store the live ones in the bottom and hang the killed ones by the hooks up near the top to cure."

"What kind of livestock is this for?"

"Whatever's handy. Can't be too picky in the last days. Now look at the time."

I followed him up the stairs to the surface. As we walked toward the car in the heat of one of the last noons to grace this civilization, a wordless suspicion sparked in my brain—not the brain that sold insurance and assessed risk for a living, but an older more primitive part, the section devoted to fearing the unfamiliar, demonizing outsiders, and intuiting the will of angry gods in every eclipse or breath of wind. It didn't take a genius to guess what type of livestock would be most numerous, most easily led when things went bad. Sheep would have the sense to run for their lives but human beings would follow Hank down the stairs into his shelter and thank him for the privilege. I'd just done it myself.

* * *

I sat on Jeff Robert and Marissa's check for days, debating with myself into the weekend. Notions of right and wrong were already eroding It was simply a question of what one could live with. But Monday afternoon I went back to the Beal residence.

The wait at the front door was considerably longer than on the previous week. I sweated through another shirt and suit, smoothed a different striped tie, and rapped the same briefcase impatiently against my leg. I noted a small fissure in the front lawn; molten earth was coming through it in slow bubbles. The Beals really ought to get that looked at.

I was on the point of pressing the bell a third time when Jeff Robert opened the door. He was wearing red pajama pants and flip flops, and his long hair, which I had never seen unponytailed, was hanging loose. It was well past noon, but he works from home. I suppose we keep different hours.

"Cousin! What can I do for you?" he said. The tone was neither hostile nor friendly. I had assumed he would invite me in—I'd been counting on that time to make my pitch—but he had no such intention. The hug was gone, too. He stood solidly in the middle of his door, waiting for me to declare my business and go on my way.

"Did I wake you?" I asked.

"No worries. What brings you by?"

"I've got to return this to you," I said, passing back the check Marissa had written me. "I can't in good conscience accept it, not from family."

"Oh Jesus Christ," Jeff Robert said, holding the check between his fingertips. "Why are you doing this to me?"

"This won't be easy for you to hear." I opened my briefcase and began to pull out the things I'd brought him, but he didn't take any notice. He was holding on to the doorframe as if for support.

"Whatever you need—whatever needs to happen to get this policy through, say the word."

"It's nothing like that. As far as the agency is concerned, everything is in order. But I feel I've deceived you. I simply can't live with myself."

"I need this policy."

"You think you do, but I assure you what you actually need are supplies. Drinking water or some way to get it. Foodstuffs. Weapons. Battery powered everything."

"I *want* what you sold me."

"You have the option of course to seek another broker, but I urge you not to do it. Under the circumstances, these policies will be worthless in short order. Spend your money on something useful—while money still has some value."

"I don't think you understand my situation. I'm in a time crunch here," he said.

"Jeff Robert, I don't think you understand *your* situation. We're all in a time crunch, man. I brought you some reading materials." I attempted to give him two books by my personal hero, Cody M. Johnson, but he wouldn't take them.

"I don't want to join your fucking church, Eric." His mistake wasn't uncommon. The Rev. Tiffany Buckle held services in a geodesic dome just down the road. Her congregation of several hundred went door to door, and they used the E.O.D. heavily in their outreach.

"I don't go to church myself," I said.

"What time is it?"

"Twelve-forty-two."

"Oh God. I have to make a phone call." He slammed his front door in my face. I left the Cody Johnsons on the mat and pocketed the check. I'd neglected to mention the fissure in his yard in the short time Jeff Robert gave me, so I jotted down a note about it:

YOU MIGHT WANT TO GET THAT LOOKED AT

with an arrow pointing to the spot. With my conscience reasonably clear, I stuck the note to the front door and went to turn in his policy, which would indeed give my monthly total a positive bump.

* * *

"Four stitches. Four stitches in her *face*," Lisa said. Our daughter Jeanette was sitting on the kitchen counter as Lisa dabbed her cheek with alcohol.

"You're sure it was Cormac? Sweetheart, look at me. Are you sure it was Cormac?"

"Yes," Jeanette sobbed. He'd dug out under the fence again and gone roaming around the neighborhood, not for the first time. But today he'd found Jeanette playing on our front porch and he'd knocked her right over and bitten her cheek. There would certainly be a scar.

"He could have killed her," Lisa said. Jeanette began to cry harder. Cormac, in spite of his owners, had always seemed a friendly enough dog, though he was also a nuisance who had a habit of wandering under my carport and spraying my tires with urine. But today something had set him off. The stitches in Jeanette's small cheek made up my mind.

"I'll go talk to them," I said, but I had no such intention. I could imagine exactly how *that* would go down, me pleading with Hank and Cerise to do the right thing, the two of them sneering, not even letting me in the door. I was tired of begging people to hear me out.

The decent thing would have been to adopt a live-and-let live strategy, to forget about Hank and his Don Cheevers, to call in a report on the dog and let the city handle it from there. Maybe fate had something deservedly unpleasant in store for Hank Schoenfeld, and if I kept my head down and played fair, we'd each get what was coming to us. *Cheaters never prosper*, as they say, despite all the evidence.

I suppose I am not a decent man, not where Hank is concerned. I hated him in a way that felt larger than myself. I hated what he stood for. I'd told Lisa that once and she'd blinked at me and said, "Well, but what does he stand for?" and then she'd turned on the blender before I could come up with an answer.

In my younger days, I would have avoided him, winced whenever our paths crossed, and gotten bitterly drunk whenever I heard of any good luck or success coming his way. But now civilization was slipping away and so were my inhibitions. His dog had sunk its teeth in my child's face. Hank had to pay.

I drove around the neighborhood a few times and when I came home I told Lisa it was all taken care of. To my surprise, she kissed my cheek. I risked draping an arm over her as we settled down to sleep that night, and for the first time all week, she didn't immediately insist I remove it.

* * *

I ate lunch early at my desk: three sandwiches and a bag of potato chips from the vending machine and as much milk as I could stand. When I was finished, I loaded my poisoned arrows in my briefcase and drove over to the Schoenfeld residence. The place was dark and locked tight as a drum, as I expected. I peered through the windows of the garage and found it empty. I walked the perimeter, sweating through my dress shirt, with the bow slung over my shoulder, looking for a weak point. It has to be done, I told myself and set my jaw. I tried to think of General Santa Anna; he'd busted a few heads in his time, and though history judged him harshly, he died at peace with his choices. That's all I wanted for myself.

I considered waiting in the yard for the dog to emerge, but it was a hundred degrees in the shade, and with my new bulky physique I was already suffering. The back entrance was fitted with a doggy door for the convenience of Cormac—the love of their dog was the one weak point in the Schoenfeld's paranoid, locked-and-loaded, kill-or-be-killed approach to life and home security.

It was almost too easy. I pushed my case of arrows through the swinging door, then my crossbow. The top half of me fit through the dog door easily, but around the middle, things began to get tight. I snaked my arm up to the doorknob and turned the lock, then I backed myself out of the door. My excess flesh scraped against the frame, and when I stood up, I was bleeding through my shirt. Then I let myself in through the unlocked door.

The noise of my entrance hadn't attracted any attention and I began to suspect that one the Schoenfelds might have taken Cormac to work. But as I walked through Hank's house looking for some sign of the dog, I heard the unmistakable sounds of a romantic interlude in progress. I froze where I stood.

"Oh, yuck," I whispered.

I'd set my mind on accomplishing a difficult and unsavory task, but even so, this was more than I'd bargained for. I covered my mouth with my hand so as to muffle the noise of my own gagging. Then I heard the sound of paws padding down the hallway. I ducked into the guest bathroom and hid behind the shower curtain, my bow armed and ready. Cormac sat down in the hall just outside the bathroom door and began licking his hind legs. I was going to kill that stupid dog, but I didn't want to take a bullet in the process. Hank and Cerise keep their firearms loaded. I could wait.

From behind the shower curtain I prepped my shot. Just when I was sure all the unpleasantness was over, it would start up again. How could these two jerks keep the passion alive when Lisa and I could barely get through dinner without an argument?

"Babe, I'm so late," Cerise said. I heard the bed springs creak as she exited. Then I heard some incidental conversation of only low interest to myself, and then a goodbye kiss of unnecessary duration and smackiness.

My God, I thought. *Was this what other people's marriages were like?* I just about sat down in the bathtub and cried, but I put aside thinking about the problem of love for the moment, and refocused on the task at hand.

A few moments later, the front door slammed. Cormac padded into the bathroom and began to lap water from the toilet. I put my finger on the trigger and carefully edged Hank's green shower curtain to the side, exposing the tip of the poisoned arrow. But I misjudged my shot. The arrow flew over the dog's head and grazed Milo, who was coming through the door wearing only a pair of athletic socks and a rose-colored sweatband.

He screamed, but he didn't know how lucky he was. There was a small abrasion on his right thigh, but it had barely broken the skin.

"Oh, Jesus," I said. "Man, I am so sorry." I kept an eye on him as I reloaded, hoping he wouldn't start spitting bubbles in his beard, but he seemed to be maintaining. I followed Cormac down the hall to the kitchen and shot him in the back leg. The poison is extremely fast acting. He fell over and began to twitch and foam at the mouth.

* * *

"I guess we both know what I'm doing here, but what are *you* doing here?" Milo said. He had grabbed Hank's camouflage robe from the hook on the bathroom door and the two of us stood over Cormac. The dog's eyes were already getting glassy.

"Also self-evident," I said. "I came to kill Hank's dog. It bit my kid's *face.*"

"Well your timing is very awkward," Milo said. He poured us each a glass of orange juice. "Next time, give me a heads up."

The pulp of the juice stuck in my teeth. "Next time? I can't kill his dog more than once. And how was I to know you were cheating on Hank?"

"*Cerise* is cheating on Hank. I'm cuckolding Hank. Big difference. Anyway, I thought you knew. She's so indiscreet," Milo said, rolling his eyes.

* * *

We agreed the best solution for all parties was that Cormac simply disappear, so we loaded him into my trunk and drove him over to the storage facility. Milo and Cerise were in love, he explained, the love of big pop ballads and great works of literature. Each Wednesday they put on jogging gear and ran from their cars, which they parked in front of the YMCA down the street, to meet at Cerise's place. He'd never felt this way before and neither had she. That I doubted. Cerise had been around the block a few times.

"She shares my beliefs. She's the only woman for me," Milo said.

"She's in the rising sea level camp, too?" If Hank knew this, he'd be almost as furious as if he knew about the other thing. But I wondered if Milo's feelings were genuine, or if he was simply resigning himself in advance to the drastically reduced dating pool of the future, which according to him would consist entirely of people who'd been aboard boats when the Gulf made its move.

* * *

Someone had scrawled

Do Not Open Till The End of Time

on the door of the Alamo Preppers communal storage unit. The idea had been that the Alamo Preppers would pool certain essential resources and keep them all in one place, in order to get the colony up and running with max efficiency during what were likely to be conditions of chaos. As Milo keyed in our code, I scanned the rows of low storage buildings. A couple of birds flew overhead in drunken loops, casting their shadows on all the blinding-white concrete. Groundsmoke blew up from some fissure I couldn't locate. It occurred to me that this would be an extremely difficult site to access once law and order rolled up the mat; there wasn't a scrap of cover.

I helped Milo push up the metal door. It took my eyes a minute to adjust and when they did, I saw the place was empty—

except for my stuff. Even Milo's things were gone. So much for the seeds, the ammonia, and the mylar we'd all chipped in for.

Milo read my thoughts. "Yeah, everybody pulled out by the end of month two. I'm keeping all my gear in the boat. Sorry buddy."

"Why didn't you say something? I feel like such an ass. I bet everyone has been laughing behind my back about this."

"No, no, no. Nothing like that," Milo said in a way that only confirmed my suspicions. He grunted with the effort of lifting the back half of the rapidly stiffening dog from my trunk.

"Careful," I said, wrapping my arms around the dog's front half. "His organs will begin to burst and you don't want dog bile on your skin." We took little shuffling half steps into the darkness of the storage unit, like two guys moving a sofa.

"Are you mad?"

"I'm humiliated," I said.

"Honest to God, I think you should be proud. It speaks well of your character that you really believed in the commune idea." Milo helped me heave the dog I'd executed onto the bare concrete floor. "Look at you. You're the total package. You're loyal. You're a great dad. Your crossbow skills are not perfect, but certainly they're decent. I mean, I'd be open to being in a flotilla with you, if you ever come to Jesus on the sea levels."

"No thanks," I said. "What now?"

"Do you want to say a few words?" I looked down at the bloated corpse of the dog that had taken a chunk from my baby girl's face.

"No."

"Then we're done. In this heat, he'll just cook down to ash."

Milo helped me load up my field toilet and MREs and then we rolled down the door on Cormac and locked it. In the road between two rows of units, a group of teens was bent over a fissure in the cement, huffing groundsmoke. Milo was young enough to simply shake his head and chuckle as he climbed in the car, but I was determined to intervene.

"What are you kids thinking?" I said. I walked over to confront them but my lungs began to burn almost at once. It's been documented that sensitivity to groundsmoke varies significantly from person to person, and I stood hacking in the smoke, trying to talk some sense into them, but hardly able to get a word out. They made quite a number of insulting personal remarks, most focused on my weight. I was getting nowhere with these jackasses and my eyes were stinging from the smoke, so I washed my hands of the situation.

When I turned back to the car, I saw that Marissa Beal was sitting on its hood. I gasped and then laughed, embarrassed by my overreaction. "Sorry cousin," I said. "What brings you here?"

"Jeff Robert brought me here," she said.

"Oh, and where is he?"

Marissa smiled and the various parts of her began to stretch and fade. The outline of her shape hung a minute in the air like the shimmer and smoke just after a firework, and then that was gone, too. There was nothing on the hood of my car but the glare.

* * *

"You should get that insured," I said to the woman behind the desk at Hyguard Property Management, Marissa's workplace. I pointed to the painting behind her head. I couldn't stop myself. I was selling relentlessly, because here in the home stretch every dollar counted, but now my goal was also just to engage her in conversation till Marissa walked through the door. My story was thin, and she hadn't yet asked outright why I was still standing at the desk and not exiting the building, but I could see it wouldn't be long.

Marissa *was* in today, her assistant explained, she was simply unavailable at the moment and anyway—she had explained this twice now, speaking very slowly as if I might be insane or not quite fluent in English—Marissa didn't handle HOA regulations. That was Marc's beat. Marc was an affable man with a knit cap and a shark tooth necklace who waved at me from his desk, but I refused to have any dealings with him. I felt the need to see Marissa with my own eyes, alive and well. "I would most definitely get that insured," I said.

"Insure *that?*" the woman said, looking at the painting behind her. Two nude cowboys strutted across the large canvas. They were standing in their stirrups, pointing their horses toward hills of cactus. Where were these cowboys going wearing nothing but their hats? How did they plan to survive *sin ropa* in the harsh climate of the Sonoran desert? A little plaque beneath it read *Galloping Nudes* by T. Crawford Picks.

"I'll get you a very good rate," I said, sliding my card across the counter and winking like I would have done in the old days. Then I blushed. I forget sometimes that I am no longer a handsome man.

She raised an eyebrow. "So like I said, I don't see that we have any complaint on file about your structure. But you haven't been permitted, so I expect it's just a matter of time before one of your neighbors blows the whistle. And then you'll get served notice from the HOA."

"And what then?"

"You can appeal. But you'll lose, eventually. And then it will have to come down." She tossed her hair, which was a lustrous dark brown. I wondered what type of shampoo she used and if it would be creepy to ask.

"Well," I said. "I'm not too worried about eventually anymore."

This caught her attention. "Parker Saenz," the woman said, introducing herself. Nobody had smiled at me that way in a long time. We shook hands. Hers was tiny, but she had an unusually strong grip, and she pressed her thumbnail into my palm in a way that meant—well, I wasn't entirely sure. Now that our business was concluded, she was appraising me according to some different criteria and I got the idea she liked what she saw.

It had been quite some time since Lisa had let her magazine drop on her bedside table and thrown a leg over mine. Our therapist, Dr. Laramie, has encouraged me to find beauty in Lisa's slovenliness, and to "make a welcome of indifference," as she put it, and I've done so as best I can, but Parker Saenz's eyes on me took my skin from flush to sizzle. I left the office in a hurry, feeling confused.

* * *

I took to sleeping in my workout clothes, wearing the key to the locker where I kept my crossbow on a chain around my neck. This did not go over well with Lisa, but I could not rest easy unless I felt that key against my skin. My crossbow was too deadly to keep casually on the garage shelf, but too necessary to secure in the backyard shelter. When the time came, I'd need it fast.

"So now you're wearing a key necklace. And you sleep in those," Lisa said, pointing to my burnt orange athletic shorts. "That's what we've come to."

"Hmmh," I said, noncommittally.

"So what's in it?"

"Baseball cards," I blurted. I spit a gob of toothpaste into the sink. God, what a stupid thing to say. The lie was transparent to the point of being insulting.

"Baseball cards." Lisa was removing her eye makeup with these little oily pads she uses. She'd accidentally smeared some under her eye like a football player, but even so, she looked pretty good.

"They're potentially valuable," I said, while my face was obscured with a washcloth .

"You're wearing the key to the locker where you keep your baseball cards—your *valuable* baseball cards that I've never heard a word about in ten years of marriage—you're wearing that around your neck all the time." She has a way of making every little thing I do seem like evidence of my so-called "mental condition."

"That's right," I said. I got into bed and pulled the quilt over my head.

"Oh hell no," Lisa said.

"What? I'm on my side." I knew better than to try to start anything romantic with Lisa while she was in her current frame of mind. I just wanted to fall asleep before she could ask any more questions.

Lisa ripped the quilt off me. "I have put up with a lot in this marriage. But I draw the line at sleeping next to a man who is wearing the key to his *baseball card* collection around his rapidly disappearing neck. Either take off the key, Eric, or go sleep on the couch."

"*Lees*," I said, but it was no use. I grabbed my pillow and headed to the couch. The sound of the bedroom door slamming echoed through our house. I settled into the cushions beneath an afghan knitted by Lisa's grandmother. On the wall opposite hung a framed candid from our wedding—the old Eric grinned at me behind a tiered cake, or rather, the young one did. He was nearly as beautiful as the bride. Both their faces were lit with elation that hadn't been seen under this roof in years.

I twirled the key at my neck. The more I tried not to think of Parker Saenz, the more I thought of her. The way her hair swung when she walked between her desk and the filing cabinet. Her thumbnail, which had left a brief crescent in my palm. Her mysterious perfume, which might well have been nothing but grocery store deodorant. I'd called the office three times, assuming different names, and each time Parker Saenz told me that Ms. Beal was unavailable to take my call. *That voice.* Of course, I knew nothing about her. But she wasn't my beloved, familiar wife, who was sickened and enraged by the sight of me. She was a stranger and she really seemed to like me. There was no future in it—but then, there was most likely no future in anything.

I pulled a book from the shelf, *The Five People You Meet in The End Times* by Cody M. Johnson, and settled back into the couch. I more or less had the thing memorized, but it was soothing to flip through it, and after a while I drifted off. But I must have been dreaming of Parker Saenz, because when I heard the key turning in the front door lock, I sat up, groggy, and whispered her name.

Parker Saenz stepped toward me through the darkness. Her hair was wild, and there was a bit of blood at her temple. She was standing in my darkened living room wearing a full skirted party dress and this could only mean one thing.

"Has it started? Am I missing it?" I began to get up from the couch but Parker put her finger to her lips and I sank back into the pillows. If we had to keep our voices down, then the clock hadn't yet run out.

"You're mine, understand?"

"Whaa?" I said, rubbing my eyes. I was almost sure I was dreaming but the next moment Parker Saenz was sitting on me. She was solid. She was radiating heat. I could hear her breathing. It was definitely happening. Parker Saenz had stolen a key to my house for the offices of the HOA and now she had come for me. She shifted slightly, driving her knee uncomfortably into my ribs, and smoothed her skirt over my lumpen blanketed form. I was too terrified to move.

"You belong to me," she whispered, punctuating each word with a rough poke of my chest. "Tell the others. Tell them not to put a hand on you."

I did not like the sound of that. "What others?" I said.

Parker Saenz smiled and began to play with the key hanging at my neck. Her free hand roamed over my chest, sort of massaging it, but painfully, grabbing handfuls of flesh and squeezing. It was very unpleasant, but I didn't want to hurt her feelings. Nor did I want to encourage her—it was all a bit terrifying, really. But sales is all about self-presentation.

"Well, it's been great to see you, Parker," I said with easy confidence, as if wrapping up some appointment we'd had, "but it's pretty late—"

She grabbed the key and pulled till the chain cut into my neck and snapped. I made a sound of protest, muffled by her strong hand over my mouth. She dangled the key over my head. "When they come, what will you tell them, Eric?"

I shrugged, or attempted to, under her weight. For a small, trim woman, she was improbably dense.

"You tell them you're mine. Understand?" She lifted her finger from my lips to let me respond.

"I understand," I said.

"Good." She dropped the key on my bare chest. "Find me on the last day. There's a place for you, Eric. But only you."

She bent low so that her dark hair fell around the sides of my face and she licked me from my stubbly chin to my temple. Then she slid off and left through the front door without another word.

I got up and turned the deadbolt in the lock. I stretched out on the couch, wiping Parker's saliva from my face with Lisa's grandma's blanket, and went back to sleep.

* * *

I sat at the breakfast table rubbing my stiff back and eating one of the low-calorie yogurts Lisa had been buying me. I'd have to stop for donuts on the way to the office, as usual. Nearly every day I stopped at the Donut Barn for a Morning Party Pack "for the office," and ate them all myself, as many as I could stand, before I pulled into the lot. The Donut Barn people probably understood I was lying, but they were professionals. They kept their hair tucked up behind netting and paper hats and they knew how to look the other way.

The girls were tromping up the stairs to get their school books and Lisa was looking at me—really looking at me for the first time in weeks.

"So your cousin Marissa—any news from her lately?" I said.

"What?" Lisa said, the way she does when a question of mine is too stupid to be dealt with. I spooned the last of the yogurt. Time to get to work. Sitting here at the breakfast table, I was just asking for trouble. The best way to stay married was to stay out of Lisa's way. I pushed my chair under the table.

"I'd at least like to know her name," she said. "The woman who was in my house last night."

I dropped my yogurt spoon into the sink. I had nearly convinced myself that Parker Saenz's nocturnal visit was a hallucination, a delayed effect of all the groundsmoke I'd huffed at the storage facility with the disrespectful teens.

"I saw you on the couch with her, under MeeMaw's blanket, no less." It was a bad sign that she wasn't hysterical. She'd been expecting something like this. I stayed out late. I made unexplained purchases. It all added up to an affair, didn't it? And now she'd seen it with her own eyes, so she thought.

"That was just Parker—she's from the HOA," I said. "She's troubled. We should change the locks, I think."

Lisa didn't respond; I had the sense that she had already chosen her words and whatever I said, she was not going to alter her little speech. "I stopped by your gym yesterday. And, funny thing, you're not a member. So why don't you tell me what you've been doing every Tuesday night. I want to know what cost us this marriage."

"Oh God," I said. If only I had joined that stupid gym. No matter how bold the plan, the smallest oversight can undo us. This was it—it was truly the end. This was the last time I would ever have breakfast with my college sweetheart, the mother of my children. I fell to my knees on the tiles. "I've been prepping again," I said.

"Oh Jesus," Lisa said. "Eric, how could you?"

"I tried to stop but, Lees, the signs are clear. The tremors, the groundsmoke, the stuff with the birds—"

She cut me off. "What happened on Y2K?"

I stared at the grout, unable to answer.

"What happened, Eric?"

"Nothing happened," I muttered.

"No. We rang in the millennium in an unheated van full of energy shakes and shotgun shells in the goddamned middle of nowhere; *that's* what happened."

I cringed at the memory. Energy shakes! I'd been such an amateur; still just a kid, really. I'd learned so much since then.

"I can't do this again. You need to leave."

"Now? You can't throw me out *now*." I wouldn't have thought it possible, but this seemed to enrage her further.

"Now's not good for you?"

"It's terrible timing. We have got to stick this out until after the—"

"Don't say it," Lisa said.

"But Lees, I promise you, we are just on the cusp—"

"I'm warning you, Eric."

"God damn it, Lisa! This thing is happening and without me, you and the girls won't last a single day!" I stood up. I was shouting. My finger was pointed right in her face—she hates that.

"Get out, Eric."

"I can't leave you Lisa. Not now."

"You will leave or I'll call Dad."

"Go ahead and call him," I said and fled the scene. We keep a pair of handcuffs in the entryway bureau. They were worn by rock legend Blaine Raddax the night he peed on the Alamo—it was the thing that brought Lisa and me together, actually. Now I snatched the cuffs and ran with them to our bedroom. I slipped one around my wrist and one around the bed post. I dropped the key between the bedframe and the wall. Elias would not be removing me from my own home without a fight.

"Goodbye girls!" I yelled as I heard them loading up for school. "Daddy loves you!"

"Goodbye, Daddy!"

As I waited for my father-in-law to show, my hand began to go numb. The handcuffs were a poor strategy, I realized. The party with greater mobility is always going to defeat the one barricaded, given enough time. Remember the Alamo? I could have kicked myself.

"You are such a dumb shit," Elias said, echoing my own thoughts. He was wearing an old guy track suit and he drank from a steaming cup of coffee. You could tell at a glance he was retired police. "What I would have done to you back in the day. A hippie like you." He sat on the edge of the bed.

"I was never a hippie," I said. "We were a metal band."

"You're still a hippie. Where's the key, Eric?"

"I swallowed it."

"I halfway believe you, Fatty. But only halfway." He finished the coffee and set it down on Lisa's bedside table. "Okay then." He lowered himself to the carpet and I could hear each individual bone creak. "Got to be here somewhere." He crawled under the bed. After a minute he inched out, holding the key in his teeth.

He was winded when he got up and I didn't have the heart to struggle. He had still been a terrifying brute the night he busted me and the Lords of Doom at the Alamo, though already somewhat past his prime. Now it was clear to me that I could have killed him just by sitting on him.

"I'll go peaceably," I said, as he unlocked the cuffs. I didn't want to humiliate the old man. Elias followed me out my own front door and we stood together in my driveway.

"So what is it this time? Maya comet?"

"Don't think so," I said, blushing. That comet thing had seemed air tight.

"What then?"

"It's the fracking, I think."

"Fracking? *Hippie*," Elias said. "What's fracking got to do with it?"

"I'm not sure," I said.

"Then what the hell are you doing this for?"

"Man, just look," I said, pointing down to the drainage ditch beneath us. A thin black smoke wafted out, slow but continuous, disappearing almost instantly as it rose in the bright air.

* * *

My own home had been off-limits to me for a week when Trip Edmonds leaned his head in my office and asked if I *had a sec*, never a good thing. I told him of course, and he settled into one of the leather horn chairs opposite my desk, grinning. There's a widely held belief among the agents of Alamo Mutual that the duration of Trip's grins is proportional to the depth of shit the grinned-at agent is in. His face was still stretched ear to ear. I feared I might soon be gathering up my things in a cardboard box.

"What can I do for you, boss?" I said.

A large black bird flew smack into the window. We both jumped at the sound, but neither of us said a word. Trip didn't even turn his head to look. All the building's windows were marked with the greasy wingprints of bird impacts, but it wasn't something we talked about. Last week at the neighbor's barbecue, while we all stood around a blazing grill, a bird—a cardinal, I think—flew right into the flames. Then it plummeted to the patio concrete and lay there, sizzling and smoking, and we all drank our beers and said nothing. After a moment somebody made an idle remark about "this time next year" and a woman kicked the bird carcass into the grass with the tip of her tennis shoe. Then people began to talk freely again, about the everyday and their nothing plans.

"I understand you're going through a rough spot," Trip said. I was sleeping every night on a foam mattress and staring up at the corrugated roof of my backyard shelter, a do-it-yourself piece of garbage I'd devoted many weekends to constructing a few years ago, for the Maya thing. When that didn't pan out, I'd sworn on anything I could think of not to prep again. I only wish Lisa understood how badly I'd wanted to keep that promise. There are preppers who long for the E.O.D., but I am not among them. If it were up to me, I'd rather the status quo.

Anyway, it certainly was not my preference to be sleeping alone in my un-air-conditioned pipe. Parker Saenz called me most nights and we talked until I fell asleep but I ignored her hints about keeping me company. I was spending every spare moment reinforcing it to withstand heat and quakes, stocking it, outfitting it with all the supplies and weapons we'd need. It was no Don Cheevers, but it was coming along. Cody Johnson's latest, *Apocalypse How? Survival Strategies for Every Budget,* was taking me through it, step by step. Lisa had said she'd rather die than spend in a night in it, but we'd soon find out one way or the other.

"Family life is complicated, Trip. But we'll figure things out," I said.

"No doubt. And you've always been a top performer here, one of the best agents in the stable. But in times like these, some people lose their heads." Trip gestured out the window, to the city of San Antonio that seethed below us. People wore paper masks and garbage bags over their clothes when they went out now, for no good reason that I could see. They just felt the need to put an extra barrier between themselves and a world that was no longer respecting its own barriers: Fault lines ran through the middle of shopping centers. Lava bubbled in suburban lawns. The earth buckled and seized and quaked, seven, eight times a day or more.

"Sometimes when people lose their heads, they also, unfortunately, make decisions that impact themselves, impact the company. I guess you know I'm talking about the Beal policy."

"Jeff Robert and Marissa," I said.

"Big policy. Real big," Trip said, crossing his leg at the knee. "Just way out of line with expected earnings. Let's call that red flag number one."

"Okay," I said.

"And they're relations of yours, yes? We'll call that red flag number two."

"That in no way impacted my thinking on the policy. They're my wife's second cousins. I don't really even consider them family, to be honest."

"Sure. Makes sense. But the trouble is—and I call this red flag number three—Marissa is as of this morning, a *very* short time after the policy kicked in, the subject of a missing person's investigation."

"Oh shit," I said.

"This surprises you?"

"Of course it does," I said. Jeff Robert—that scheming bastard. He'd sat at his kitchen table and lied to me. He'd even teared up when we talked about funeral expenses. I was going to swing him around by his pony tail when I found him. I'd all but painted a target on his wife's back and now whatever he'd done I was paying for it, too.

"Because I read faces, and I would say yours, right at this moment? Surprise is not the feeling I'm getting." Trip's admin, Crystal, came in with an empty box. "Right on time," Trip said, grinning.

* * *

Our whole neighborhood was plastered with signs.

LOST DOG REWARD IF FOUND

Cormac's face looked out at me from every telephone pole. *Friendly, Loving Pup* the flyer said. I shook my head in disgust. Jeanette's stitches had come out, but the puckered red marks left by Cormac's teeth still oozed and stung. It brought tears to her eyes to have the wound cleaned.

I drove home with the contents of my desk in a box on the passenger seat. A much younger and happier Lisa and the two baby girls smiled in the photo on the top of my box. Whatever else I did or didn't bring to the table, I'd always brought my paycheck. Lisa had never been able to reproach me for that.

I pulled under the carport and slammed the door. I believe in keeping a positive attitude but I saw no silver lining here. I opened the lid of the garbage can and hurled the box down into it.

"Bad day, neighbor?" Hank said. He was standing square in the middle of my lawn with his arms crossed over his chest. The shirt he had on was sleeveless and a large bandage pad was taped over one of his impressive biceps.

"Real bad," I admitted.

"Same here," Hank said, but he smiled about it, as if he were kind of enjoying himself.

"Are you hurt?" I asked pointing to his arm.

"Not where you can see," Hank said, but he began peeling the tape off the top edge of the bandage to show me anyway.

"Want a beer?" I suggested.

"Love one. As long as you don't have to go in the house for it."

"The house is where we keep them."

"Oh, we better hold off then. I'm here to make sure nobody goes in to that house until it's safe to do so." Hank pulled the bandage away from his arm. I didn't make a sound; I just took it all in and began to calculate my odds of escape. They weren't good.

"What's going on, Hank?" I said. "Have you been talking with Milo?" There was a fresh tattoo on his bicep, a dog's head in profile. A large tear dropped from its eye.

"I went by the Alamo Prepper's storage unit this morning."

"But why would you?" I said, trying to contain my horror.

"That's not important. But I guess you know what I found there. Anyway, first thing I did was give that poor dog a proper burial. Next thing, I went to INKitUP! to have something made to honor him. He was the best goddamned dog."

"Cormac was dangerous."

Hank held up a hand. "Don't speak his name. I don't want to hear his name on your lips. You fat coward." I didn't see what fat had to do with it. Fat was a temporary, fluctuating matter of body mass that had no bearing on my character either way, but people always seemed to throw it in when they wanted to be insulting.

"So I sat there in the chair with tears streaming down my face while a green haired kid with a nose ring cut into my arm and I asked myself *who?* Who would do such a thing? What miserable son of a bitch would kill that dog and dishonor his corpse that way? And then I remembered *you*, the biggest joke in the entire AP group. Your pathetic little port-o-potty wasn't there, because you took it out and then you stuck my dog in there to rot."

"He bit my kid's face, Hank."

"That's bullshit. Cormac never hurt the innocent. He just didn't have it in him. But I'm sure he gave you a fight the day you took his life."

"Actually no," I said, brushing past him. "And I'm going in my house now."

"Oh no. Too risky. I want you alive." Hank wrapped his arms around me, restraining me.

"Excuse me?"

Hank was a protein-shake-swilling, bench-pressing monster. I struggled, but I immediately saw there was no way I could break out of his grasp.

"I can't risk you getting hurt by a stray bit of shrapnel," Hank said, spitting in my ear as he spoke. "I don't want a scratch on you. I want you in perfect health so that when the day comes, you won't have any excuse. And now you won't have anything to help you either—no shelter, no supplies. Nothing but your own stupidity and weakness."

"You asshole," I said. And then the explosion knocked us both off our feet.

* * *

The sky was the wrong color. The grass beneath me pressed its sharp blades into my back and there was a roaring in my ears just as Milo had said there would be when the yellow-brown Gulf poured into our neighborhoods and drowned us all. I was stretched out on my front lawn, watching big gray puffs of smoke blow over the roof of my house. Hank Schoenfeld had blown up our shelter.

* * *

Hank was long gone when I dragged myself off my lawn and into the house. The panes of the windows that faced the yard had been blown out. I swept up the glass and stared out the empty window frame into my lawn. There was a medium-sized, smoking pit in my backyard and some scattered debris, nothing useable. I took a beer from the refrigerator and began to board up the back windows. I felt an odd sort of peace. I had no supplies, and without a job, no means to replace them. I had nothing but my wits, which I was now dulling with as much beer as I could hold. When I finished the job, I put the hammer on the coffee table and stretched out on the couch.

* * *

The texts woke me. It was the worst day of my life: I had a serious beer headache at two-thirty in the afternoon, there was a smoking pit in my backyard, and I was unemployed. The prospect of bringing Lisa up to speed on all this was more than I could bear to contemplate. Worse yet, I remembered, as I sat up on my couch and fumbled for my phone, while my living room spun around like a carnival ride, my reputation was in tatters. By now it was all up and down Alamo Mutual that I had been complicit in some kind of an insurance crime. I'd walked out with as much dignity as I could muster, but the cardboard box in my arms made it all too clear that I'd been canned.

And yet, in spite of all this, my phone was lighting up with texts that were oddly congratulatory, many from industry contacts. *You called it, man!*

I responded with some ambiguous emoji, not knowing what to make of these messages and not wanting to set people straight either. That would come later. My head hurt too much now. I stared out our picture window. A thin stream of groundsmoke was blowing over the roofs of the houses. Lisa and the girls were getting out of the car. She was still in a workday blazer, with her hair tied up in a way I have always especially liked. It broke my heart a little. In profile she looked younger, like the vivacious girl in a college sweatshirt I remembered. The woman now walking up to my front door weighed herself daily and watched the balance on our credit card creep always in the wrong direction and had walked in on her husband sharing Mee-Maw's blanket with a stranger. The difference between the two Lisas wasn't simply time; the difference was me. I had taken the life out of her somehow, and I was about to do it again.

"Hi Daddy!" the girls screamed. I kissed them both as they ran upstairs to the playroom, shedding school books and lunchboxes, socks and shoes, all over the living room.

"Eric?" Lisa said looking me over. I had no way of knowing how much of my day was obvious just at a glance, but she didn't immediately demand my exit from the house.

"I have some news," I said, following her into our bedroom — hers now, really — as she hung up the blazer and stepped out of her uncomfortable shoes. The phone in my pocket kept buzzing.

"Is that yours or mine?"

"Mine. But it's not important."

"Wait — it's mine, too," Lisa said and pulled her phone from her purse. I didn't wait; it was easier to tell her without eye contact.

"Lisa, I don't have a job anymore."

"Oh my God," Lisa said, looking at her phone. "You were right."

"Can we focus on this conversation for a minute? I got fired today, Lisa."

"Of course you did," Lisa said. She was in the grip of some strong emotion, but to my surprise, it didn't seem to be rage or pain. She put her hands on my face and kissed me on the lips. "Thank God you never listen to me."

I was disoriented by my midday drinks and my wife's random burst of passion for me. I should have asked more questions but I didn't, not till I was lying beside her in our bed completely winded, wondering how long it would take to get back in shape.

"So this is all over," Lisa said. Her eyes were filling with tears.

"What?" I said, sitting up in bed. Maybe it was *not* a good sign what had just happened. Maybe it was some sort of sentimental preface to being served with divorce papers.

"What does this mean for us? What's your plan? I'm afraid," Lisa said, and she burst into tears. I put an arm around her.

"Lisa, I'll do whatever it takes to save us. And that starts with no more prepping. The shelter is gone. The supplies are gone. And I don't even care. I'm through with all that. Never again." I was having a beer- and explosion-induced epiphany. I couldn't prepare for the collapse of civilization; all I could do was spend each discrete twenty-four hour period that came to me trying to make things work again. Lisa and me and our girls—the important thing was that if we were all going down in flames, we were going together.

"Are you kidding?" Lisa said. I grabbed her hand and pressed it to my heart.

"I have never been more serious," I said.

"You don't have a generator or MREs or anything. It's all gone?"

"Every last bit," I promised. I began to give her a rundown of the events she'd missed while we weren't speaking, beginning with my assassination of Cormac.

"Well that is just *priceless*." Lisa said, through her sobs. Our phones were migrating toward the edge of the nightstand from all the buzzing. I grabbed mine before it took a dive and began to read through the odd texts that had so puzzled me earlier with a clearer head. Friends, family, and colleagues had sent dozens of messages about major statewide earthquakes, a chain running from the panhandle to the Rio Grande. Volcanic activity had forced the evacuation of Austin, and an enormous sinkhole sucked up a swath of the northern suburbs of Dallas. Some were asking after my safety, others congratulating me for predicting the enormous state-wide disaster now at hand, and I had evidently replied to them all with the image of a disco dancer, some fireworks, and an obese cat riding a scooter.

"It's finally happening," I said. On the one hand, it was the day I had prepped for, the day I had promised was coming, *the day I had warned about till I was blue in the face*. I tried not to let that go to my head; this was a human tragedy and there was no time to strut and crow and say *I told you so*.

On the other, of course, I myself now had absolutely no preparations in place. Thanks to Hank, I was no better off than the nay-sayers who'd lived with their heads in the sand, in terms of provisions and supplies. The feelings I was feeling then could only ever be understood by a person who has been right all along but who then comes to find out that *having absolutely called it* in fact does them no good whatsoever.

* * *

Lisa evicted me from the bedroom and closed herself up in there with a bottle of wine. I put the girls to bed and spent the night formulating a Plan B in light of these new circumstances. In the morning, I shaved my face carefully for the last time and slapped my cheeks with aftershave. It was a new world, and I was a new man. And so right at the opening bell of this new order, I promised myself to live with absolute honesty. And more than myself, I promised Lisa.

I opened the door to my bedroom, which Lisa had left unlocked, I was encouraged to find. She was lying under the quilt, crying softly, while the doings of the president and other heads of state were reported by the last remaining local news outlet. So-called experts talked nonsense about keeping calm and sheltering in place.

If Lisa heard me come in, she gave no sign. I let my towel drop on the carpet and approached her nude, so as to underscore my point: naked honesty. I looked into her eyes and I said, "Lisa, no more lies. From now on, I'm going to be totally, completely honest with you."

She was about eye-level with my midsection, which is not as toned as it once was and she gave it a cold, judging look. "I don't even know if I *want* to apocalypse with you," she said. It was like it made no difference to her, the fact our whole way of life was over. She hadn't altered her attitude toward me even the smallest bit.

I took a deep breath, keeping my rage in check. We had bigger problems than our problems, but trust Lisa not to get that. "I think we better get Dr. Laramie on the phone," I said. Since I'd moved into the shelter, we'd been seeing our therapist twice a week. "And then we'll load up the girls and go over to Blaine's."

She sat up in bed. "Blaine's? *That's* your big doomsday plan? Un-be-*lieve*-able." I thought that was a pretty interesting choice of words from a person who hadn't believed any of this would even happen.

* * *

Dr. Laramie didn't pick up, so I left a message apprising her of the scene in the bedroom and asking for a callback at her earliest convenience. I rousted Jeanette and Annabelle and scrambled them some eggs, which they picked at. A car alarm was sounding in the near distance and from one or two streets over, a beagle howled. All over Texas people were pouring coffee and wrapping their heads around the situation, which meant time was short.

"Toilet, teeth, clothes, hair, socks and shoes, girls," I said. "Fast motion." Jeanette sprang from the table just like we drilled it, but I had to carry Annabelle upstairs and walk her through the entire morning routine.

"What about Mommy?" Annabelle said as I buckled her into her booster. Lisa has never participated in any of our drills, but I swore to my girls that *when it counted* she'd be there with us. Now it was time to put my personal ambivalence about their mother aside and make that happen.

"Mommy's coming. Stay put, you two." Back in the house, I kept my tone positive. "Lisa," I called. "It's time to go, honey." No response. The only sound was the bathtub filling. I got a running start and rammed the door with my body.

"It wasn't locked, *Eric.*" She has this way of saying my name—if you belong to a hated minority group, you'd definitely recognize the tone. There were bubbles in the tub and scented candles along the side. I clutched my chest. "I thought you were taking a Roman exit," I said. "Oh thank God. Thank God you're okay."

Lisa rolled her eyes. She's always so cool, that's what gets to me. Still soaping her feet like I hadn't just busted down the door.

"Lisa, in a civilization-ending event, the initial stasis is quickly followed by a period of widespread violence. For instance, when the Visigoths arrived on the outskirts of Rome in A.D. 410, for the first 48 hours they just barbecued and played wind instruments—"

"Don't get pedantic with me, you son of a B," Lisa said, grabbing her bathrobe. We implemented a strict no-cursing rule in our home when Jeanette was born, and despite our ups and downs as a couple, we've both stuck with it.

"You're going in that?" I said.

Lisa was padding toward the garage in her bathrobe and slippers. "It's the end of the world. F it."

* * *

Stockpile weapons and foodstuffs. Then hole up in the country, away from major urban centers. That's how you come out on the sunny side of apocalypse, right? Common misconceptions. As we drove through downtown toward Blaine's, I observed litter in the streets, and roving groups of men, two or three strong, likely to snowball into death squads within a 72 hour period. But I had to chuckle at some of the beginner mistakes I was seeing. At the corner of Commerce and Main, a man in bicycle gear was trying to buy some fruit stand melons with gold bullion.

I rolled down my window. "Sir!" I called. "Excuse me, sir! You'll want to hang on to that bullion until stage three." The man whipped around. He was big and lean, the absolute worst body type for even a short-term famine. I'm not a tall man, and I'd been strategically gaining weight as the storm clouds gathered, while Lisa is naturally pear shaped.

"*Cody Johnson?*" I said. It was only eight in the morning, but I knew nothing that happened on this historically surprising day would shock me more.

"Eric Estrada," he said. You've got to hand it to him, he's good with names. We'd only met the one time, when he came to address our preppers group.

"Yes! Man, I have read every single one of your books. Huge fan."

Cody leaned into the window. His eyes were bleary. "You told me that night at the Cracker Barrel—an ear bending I won't soon forget. I've got to move this bullion," he said. His breath reeked of Midori. "One bar, five cantaloupe. My final offer." The vendor shook her head; no fool she.

"Mr. Johnson," I said, for the man was clearly in distress, "We've got to get you sobered up. Hop in." Lisa was making slicing, nix-it motions across her neck, but Cody Johnson is one of my personal heroes. If my family and I survive this thing, it'll be mostly because of him.

"So you can rob me of my gold, make me your slave, then feed on my flesh when your provisions run short?"

I laughed, but Cody Johnson was serious. He turned back to the fruit vendor. "Two bars, five cantaloupe, and I'll throw in my windbreaker." The vendor nodded and began bagging up the fruit. That was it. I pressed on the hazard lights and stepped out of the car.

"Cody, bullion is a failed strategy. You know this. It's declining in value as we stand here." The vendor was still holding the paper bag. "*And* your shirt," she said. Cody pulled off his shirt.

"Wait!" I said. "This isn't how this works. You hold your bullion until the new order emerges, and then you find yourself a potentate. Nobody else has any use for gold—there's no intrinsic value there; just window dressing. But a potentate needs to advertise her power, and that's where your bullion comes in. People will say, 'Well, shit. That lady's got herself some gold. She must be making out all right. Better not rise against her or take her generator, or I'll get a boot in the ass... she'll crush me.' Do you see?"

The vendor nodded. "I'll need the shoes, too," she said.

"Why are you doing this?" Cody said.

A bit of soot drifted down onto my t-shirt and I brushed at it. "Because your books touched my life. Your books are the reason I'm ready for this day."

"You want to make a necklace out of my bones, is that it?"

"Mr. Johnson. Cody... Cantaloupe is highly perishable! What are you thinking?"

"I've got a craving," Cody said. "I want to bite into the flesh of a sweet melon just one more time before I die." The vendor began to slice open the melons with a large curved knife.

Keep emotions in check; that's the ground level of seeing your way through doomsday. But I had already had to deal with disrespect and non-compliance in the heart of my own family and my fuse was short. I got in Cody Johnson's face. "You coward! You're a disgrace to the movement," I said.

And that's when Cody Johnson demonstrated that he might still have what it took to make it. He grabbed the vendor's knife and in one fluid motion, he raised the blade and brought it down on my thigh, slicing it open. I hobbled back into the car and put it in drive.

"That's probably going to abscess," Lisa said, as blood poured down my pant leg. I checked the mirror to see if Cody Johnson was going to chase us, but he was standing on the corner, naked but for a tiny pair of bicycle shorts, his arms full of cantaloupe.

* * *

Halfway to Blaine's a call comes in, and it's not Dr. Laramie. It was Parker Saenz. Our emotional affair had now raged for seven tortured days, though out of respect for Lisa, I'd refused to get physical.

"I guess that makes you a hero," Lisa said, and I had to blush, because I'd been thinking out loud again. It was a habit I'd developed during the separation, all those lonely hours in my empty shelter. I switched both phone and internal monologue to silent. Hero? No, it doesn't make me a hero per se, and yet, there are things *less heroic* than withstanding a relentless and highly sophisticated campaign for one's sexual attention.

For instance, right now, with the social order collapsing, when a certain slippage of standards is inevitable, even necessary, was I running to the muscular arms of Parker, who both respects and desires me? Nope. I was letting that phone buzz forlornly on the console. Because once, under an arbor of plastic lilies, I'd promised to love only Lisa. I'd finger-fed her white cake from H-E-B. And now I was going to get through this thing or die trying, probably the latter, with the woman who, despite not having bothered to brush her hair this morning, was regarding *me* with 100 proof scorn.

If the atmosphere inside the sedan was tense, it was nothing compared to the situation in the streets. The rate of illegal u-turns, jaywalking, red-light-running and tailgating increased with a relentless doomsday rapidity, traffic laws being the first to go. We nearly head-onned a charter bus that made an illegal left onto our one-way street, and I began to worry we'd left it too late, having lost precious minutes while Lisa took a bath, a goddamned *bath*, in the middle of our evac protocol. I felt myself floundering toward another go-round with the blame-anger-remorse cycle, but per Dr.

Laramie I took a deep inhale and imagined Lisa as someone deserving of love and protection, like a vulnerable baby panda.

"Well anyway, it's a beautiful sky," I said to the baby panda. She had dark circles of yesterday's makeup around her eyes, which made the panda thing more workable.

"It's blood-red, *Eric*," the Lisa/panda said, as if there could only be one valid perspective here. Lisa's seat was in max recline position and her feet were resting up on the dash. I recalled that I had not actually witnessed her put on underwear, and in fact there was little reason, given her current state of mind, to suspect she'd bothered with such niceties. But you apocalypse with the spouse you have, and so I refused to let her bare- and half-assed efforts weaken my resolve.

"Take a good look, girls. You'll want to tell your grandchildren about this one day," I said, referring, of course, to the shocking Armageddon hue of the horizon, and not to Lisa's pantslessness. But their innocent faces were pressed against the glowing screen of their KidMinders. It was probably for the best. Birds were beginning to drop from the trees along the Riverwalk in clumps of sticky black feathers, and this amped up the panic level on the street.

I determined that now was the opportune moment to dispense with the speed limit, though I advised the girls that when they came of age in the new order, I would not want to hear of them hot-rodding around in any such manner. The remaining miles to Blaine's were covered at maximum speed possible for a mid-range four-door family sedan in a near chaos scenario.

* * *

The apocalypse doesn't discriminate. Rich or poor, when push comes to shove, it doesn't make a bit of difference who you are. That's the conventional wisdom. But I was betting that it *would* discriminate: cities might be levelled, but the playing field wouldn't be, which was why we'd left our own neighborhood for Blaine's and were bluffing our way into his loft.

"Erik Estrada?" The security guards at Blaine's building peered at me with awe and confusion. "*The* Erik Estrada?" As predicted, the brewing unrest had yet to reach the city's tonier districts, which is why the guards were lolling around with machine guns at half-mast.

"That's right," I said. Lisa gave me a look, as if I weren't saving her life and the lives of our children with this simple subterfuge. Do not think that trading off the name of a middling celebrity thirty years older than myself has gained me a life of undeserved privilege, because it has not. Has it, on occasion, proved useful? Certainly.

"Huge fan," the burlier of the guards said, opening the gate. When we were safely on the inside I leaned into his ear and whispered, "Now would be the time to initiate Protocol X."

"Alexis, he's calling it."

"Can he do that?" This from the less burly colleague. I smiled in a way that broadcast authority, and the two of them conferred. "Well, Jesus. I guess we'd better." With a faint mechanical hum, Protocol X went live.

* * *

Blaine Raddax came to the door wearing a vest and a pair of leather pants. He had on a number of studded leather bracelets and a tattoo of a skull with eagle wings took the place of a shirt. He looked like the rock god he was, and immediately I felt self-conscious on behalf of the entire Estrada crew. Lisa looked like a heroin addict, but without the svelteness so often associated with that condition. She was basically nude and possibly not entirely sober. The girls were wearing the first things they'd pulled from their drawers. I had not thought to check whether they matched. They didn't. The little one had her shoes on the wrong feet. My too-tight pants were also an inch too short, one leg was blood soaked, and the waistband was cutting a red band into my belly. In short, the Estradas were starting at rag-tag; our only hope was that the rest of the survivors would sink rapidly to our level.

"So this is your family," Blaine said.

"Sure is," I said. I shrugged in kind of a *what can you do?* manner. He ushered us in the door. Blaine was once an insurer's nightmare, a liability who walked the earth in leather pants, smashing collectible guitars, trashing hotel rooms, wrecking expensive vehicles. But he'd mellowed with age. Now Blaine's passion was art; he collected mostly outsize paintings of jungle cats or attractive women posing with or like jungle cats. I heard Lisa snort at the art that lined his walls. I elbowed her; good manners only become more important when the fabric of society begins to fray. Luckily Blaine did not notice her rudeness.

Blaine's loft is only one of his residences and I tried not to focus on its opulence and on what might have been, how my family and I might be tucked safe and secure in an impenetrable luxury condo of our own instead of crashing here, house guests in Blaine's downtown loft. But I'd quit the band when I met Lisa, who didn't care for percussion, and sold my drum kit and tasseled leather gloves to attend Alamo U with her. The Lords of Doom had gone on to fame without me, and when metal started to seem like a joke they retired. At thirty.

The girls began leaping between Blaine's velvet chaise and leopard print sofa with bizarre animal shrieks, like they were completely keeping pace with the collapse of manners and customs that was raging in the streets below us.

"Girls! Operation Silent Night!" I said. The girls stopped, dropped, and stretched out on the flokati, feigning sleep, with only minimal giggling.

* * *

Blaine used to tutor me in Algebra, but years of the rock and roll lifestyle had left him slow on the uptake. "This whole thing is going to blow over in 24 hours. Twenty four hours *max*. We're going to laugh about this someday," he kept saying. I had squeezed into a pair of Blaine's suede shorts and was wrapping my leg in gauze. I needed stitches, and without the adrenaline that had gotten me through the drive over, the pain was becoming considerable.

"Most of Dallas is gone. They've abandoned Austin," Lisa said. "I know it's hard to believe that *Eric* was right, but a lot of people have lost their lives. The least you can do is acknowledge what's happening. Show some respect."

After so many years of denial, I felt gratified to hear Lisa acknowledge the truth about the civilizational disasters I'd so long predicted, but I wished she wouldn't take that tone with our host.

Blaine twisted his long hair into a loose topknot. "Look, man. I've toured the world. I've played sold out shows in Stockholm and Tokyo. I'm not what you would call the quote-unquote average citizen. And I've learned to be cynical, okay? What they say—that's not the real story. All of this, everything you think you've seen, has been engineered to keep us from questioning our leaders."

"There are no leaders anymore," I pointed out. Last night, the President had found it to be a convenient moment to grant one of the petitions for secession we were always sending up to D.C. We were a republic again, for two and a half glorious hours, before our leaders had been forced to evacuate the Texas capitol.

"Oh, aren't there?" Blaine said. "Think about that man. Think about what you just said. The puppet masters have got you exactly where they want you."

* * *

"Holy shit," Blaine said. "Holy shit." The three of us were listening to the intermittent broadcasts on my shortwave radio, or rather, Blaine and I were listening. Lisa had fallen asleep on the couch. She was snoring softly and drooling on one of Blaine's throw pillows and I was ashamed of her, though I tried not to let Blaine see it. I saw him looking at my wife of ten years and feeling vindicated in his choices, which were mostly very short term arrangements with "girls who liked to party."

Jeannette and Isabel had opened the doors of Blaine's mirrored closets and were dressing themselves in the studded leather and feathery coats he wore when he played arena shows.

"Turn it up," Blaine said. On the radio, they were calling it a regional disaster, but concern was mounting that it might not just be Texas that was going down in flames. For hours we'd had to endure smug chickens-coming-home-to-roost narratives put out by the coastal chatterers, but the scale of the disaster had shut them up. The same jerks who couldn't hide their satisfaction in watching the Lone Star state go down in flames were now weeping on air for the "fate of all humanity," etc. Because now it wasn't just Wal-Mart shoppers and men in camo sweats and fishing glasses who were freaking. The panic was spreading. Whatever was happening, it was dire. Frantic scientists of uncertain credentials speculated that a major disruption had occurred in earth's core and now perhaps our entire planet was undergoing geologic death, just leaking out its energy like a dying battery. The industry put out a statement calling for the end of the finger-pointing. This was all just part of a natural process. I wasn't sure they were wrong, the industry shills. The dinosaurs had been blasted from the face of the earth by a natural process, so who was to say?

The leading theory seemed to be that the earth was just going to shut down and go cold after all the pyrotechnics and shaking were done; these death throes might stretch between several weeks or a hundred or more years. It was as vague as a delivery window, but the product we were all waiting on was total planetary death.

"We're all going to die," Blaine said.

I shushed him. "The girls," I whispered. "And anyway we *might not* die."

"No, it's over. This is truly the end of the road. But I'm ready," Blaine said. "I have prepared for this day."

"You have?" I said. I hoped he meant in a practical way, and not just spiritually, because I didn't care for the thought of being subjected to a lot of prayer beads and chanting or what have you.

Blaine left the room. I followed. "Do you have MREs or weapons or what?" Foresight was typically the first brain function destroyed by regular drug use. The long ago night when he'd peed on the Alamo, there was already evidence of his inability to anticipate consequences and prepare for the future. And Blaine had worked his way through an ocean of narcotics and amphetamines between that night and the one, years later, his rock bottom moment, when his heart stopped inside a Vegas strip club. They'd shocked him back to life in front of the buffet and he'd been clean and sober ever since.

"Better than that, my friend. First let me get Andrea," he said.

"You can't open the door, Blaine!" We were safe, or safe-ish high above the streets, behind a door of industrial strength steel, but it was no time to go traipsing through the hallways. Protocol X meant that nobody would be allowed in or out of the building until the all clear sounded. But soon enough the guards would realize the all clear was *never* going to sound; they would be abandoning their posts to go to their own families at any moment, if they hadn't already, and then our best hope was to hunker down until the dust settled.

"Relax," Blaine said. "Careful with your weapon, I've got breakables in here." I stood in the doorway with an arrow primed as Blaine went out into hall in his bare feet and knocked on the door across the way.

* * *

"Don Cheevers. Let me tell *you* something about Don Cheevers," Andrea said. She had owned a high-end real estate company back when there was a housing market and her contempt for the Cheevers brand of luxury shelters was absolute. "I wouldn't buy anything from that guy. I mean, nothing. I wouldn't even buy, I don't know... Like I wouldn't even buy—"

"Drugs," Blaine suggested, wiping his nose.

"Exactly. I wouldn't buy *drugs* from Don Cheevers."

Like many recovering addicts, Blaine kept a doomsday stash. That was the extent of his preparations. Initially I'd been disgusted by this, by the cynical hedonism of it, but once I'd agreed to join them, I had more respect for this decision. I'd forgotten how drugs made you feel—divorced from all your failures, and like your most hopeless day was still the best party ever. But I'd done only enough to be civil and to take the edge off the agony of my hacked-up thigh, while the girls were busy eating cookies and watching Bugs Bunny cartoons from Blaine's video library. Lisa was still asleep.

"Well, okay. But answer me this—who *did* you buy drugs from?"

"My stylist," Andrea said.

"But who did he buy it from? From a terrible person. And who did that person buy it from? From some sick psychopathic narco son of a bitch. This is murder powder," I said, pointing to the coffee table where Blaine was divvying out more lines. "None for me, thanks," I added. "Andrea, innocent people died so that you could paint your nostrils white. You're snorting up human misery. You're a person without scruples, a woman who will overlook the most horrific violence and criminality in the interest of fulfilling her own petty pleasures. And yet you're telling me, *you* wouldn't buy from Don Cheevers *on principle*?"

"That's right," Andrea said. "Believe me he is bad news. We had a thing—it was years ago. But there are two words for that man: con artist." Andrea began to tick off his flaws on her long nails. "He doesn't build to code. He's a liar. And the money—"

"Follow the money. Always follow the money," Blaine said. The two of them burst into hysterical laughter. I didn't get it. They were connecting on some plane I couldn't reach due to my comparatively modest intake, and I felt left out.

Lisa sat up on the couch and took in the scene. "What the F, Eric," she said. "This is your plan?" I didn't like the way she was looming over the coffee table.

"*Calmate*, Lees," I said.

"This is your plan for us?"

"Lisa don't!" But she was already doing it. She flipped over the coffee table. Powder filled the air and Andrea screamed.

"Nobody move!" Blaine yelled as the powder descended over his living room set; and then, "Get the broom!"

"Jeanette! Isabel! Let's go!" The girls appeared instantly, having correctly deduced from her tone that their mother was at max rage and meant business. Jeanette was wearing some sort of leather overalls and a denim and rhinestone cap; Isabel had on a golden cape and a dog collar and purple boots that reached her thighs.

"Babe," I said. That was the drugs talking. I hadn't called her babe in years. "Go? Go where?"

"Anywhere," Lisa said. "I'd rather be out there than in here with these people."

* * *

I followed them out to the empty street pleading with Lisa to get back in the building but she walked barefoot down the sidewalk, the belt of her bathrobe trailing behind her, holding each of our girls by the hand, not even turning her head. I was following behind them, a yelling fat man with a crossbow, when I realized that the streets were not entirely empty. The sound of a big wheeled vehicle could be heard one to two streets over, though I couldn't see it through the office buildings. It made me nervous. "Lisa, it's not safe out here," I pleaded.

I estimated that the death squads were just gearing up, sort of dipping their toes in. They were doing a little window smashing, some shooting out of traffic lights, waiting to see if there would be any response. It was becoming clear there wouldn't be. A sheriff's department car was parked street side. Someone had fed the meter, but the car's door was open, its blinker signaling left. The scanner let off blank bursts of static and a classic Haggard played through the speakers *think I'll just stay here and drink.*

"Lisa, where are you going?" I said. Lisa stepped over the shards of a window. Paper blew out through the hole in the glass. A funny thing—peripheral vision remains acute even when a person is too blind to find their own glasses on the bedside table without fumbling. Such a person will still be able to detect movement. For instance, the house cat that stalks over the blankets will register as a threatening blur. It's because death has a way of sidling up to us; always has. I saw the man step from the corner and raise his bat, but I was a forty-year-old, recreational drug using fat man, and my instincts were dull. I just stood there and let him bring the bat down on my skull.

* * *

I woke up tasting asphalt. My tongue had lolled out of my mouth and I carefully retracted it back behind my dry, bloody lips. Inches from my eyes I saw the ridged soles of a hiking boot.

"Lisa?" I said.

I lifted my head and called for her again, knowing she was gone. I stood up, swaying. At my feet was a teen in an inspirational shirt: Together Everyone Achieves More. Go Mules! Somehow, I had taken my assailant down with me, and this salvaged a bit of my respect, but only a bit, because he was very young, and if his shirt was credible, only a junior varsity member of the swim team.

I slapped his cheek to wake him and found it cold. His bat was lying in the street and his hands were convulsed around my crossbow. I deduced that he'd accidentally shot himself in the chest at point blank range. I pried my crossbow from his cold, dead fingers and removed the arrow from his chest. It made a sick, sucking sound upon exit. Then I picked up the bat, wiping my own blood—and brains, for all I knew—onto my shorts and hobbled down the street. I wasn't entirely sure I was alive anymore.

The longer I walked, the less certain I became that I wasn't back there in the street with my head split open. A woman in a yellow hat was raising herself out of an open manhole. "They're down here, darling. *General!* Everybody is down here."

She kept speaking to me out of the smoke that blew up around her, but I kept my eyes away from hers. Dead or not, I knew better than to linger. The manhole began to spit a geyser of molten ooze. I climbed the fire escape of the nearest building. My feet were unsteady on the narrow steps. The street below me filled with fire, the sky blew down ash, and I was dizzy. I dragged myself onto the tar and gravel roof and collapsed.

II

"Do you know the expression 'let bygones be bygones'?" Trip Edmonds said. He was wearing a toga made of orange tarp, belted with an electrical cord, and as he spoke, he cinched the belt tighter around his ever shrinking waist. He was so hungry he chewed little twigs and handfuls of leaves from the live oak trees when he thought nobody was looking. The lean muscle mass people were really having a bad time of it.

"Of course," I said. "But that guy—"

"That's what I'm living by in these latter days. Bygones be bygones, or *B.B.B.* That's the reason I took you on, gave you your own sector. Now if you can't pay that forward, well..."

Trip looked up at the shattered Captain Burger sign that marked the community's northern boundary and shook his head. Behind him, Human Resources was doing some military type drills, marching and spinning their guns in sync. "We're building something from the ground up here, in every possible sense—and I think it's important that we're all reading from the same playbook. I want to incubate a forward-looking culture. We don't have the luxury of Monday morning quarterbacking, not in these times. Were mistakes made? No doubt about it. But I guess the thing I keep coming back to, Eric, is that *we've all done things we're not proud of.*"

I looked over to where Jeff Robert, that ponytailed bastard, stood wearing rainboots and a pair of paint-splattered overalls, waiting to learn his fate. "Yes," I conceded. "But we did those things after. He did his thing *before*."

I'd pushed it too far. Trip was grinning like his face would split in half. "I seem to recall that there was some question of your involvement in the thing before. You say you didn't have a hand in it; well, Jeff Robert also says he had no hand in his wife's disappearance. I choose to believe you both, though I can't know with anything like scientific certainty that you and he are not guilty of murder and fraud and what have you. All I do know is that you are two healthy, able bodied males between the ages of 18 and 50, the prime demographic for this industry. So can you work together, or are we going to have a problem?" I could see the man's cheek bones jutting out beneath his thin, sagging skin as he grinned at me.

"B.B.B," I said. Trip clapped me on the shoulder with one of his bony hands and I went to welcome Jeff Robert to the team.

"Look, asshole," I said, handing him a canvas sack. "You fill your quotas and stay out of my way." Jeff Robert took the sack and followed the others.

My team of product reclamation specialists was working a strip mall north of the loop today—a hot, dangerous walk over many treeless miles without any cover to speak of. He had no weapon, and I sure as hell wouldn't be lending him one from my small arsenal. With any luck, a rider would get him or he'd step onto a lava geyser and I wouldn't have to work with the likes of him again. Otherwise, Marissa's ghost was definitely going to be on my case about it.

We preferred not to call ourselves garbage pickers, but that's what we were. We sorted through the rubble for useful refuse from the old civilization. It was a dirty job, but I was good at it, number two in my territory, just beneath Trip Edmonds, who was—well, the man was just a garbage picking *machine*. I'd always assumed his dominance over me in the insurance field was due to pure dumb luck, and so it was galling to come second to Trip in yet another field, under the auspices of a new civilization. But I had to confess it was a thing of beauty, the way he worked. The man had an eye like a crow. He could spot a useable tennis racket or scrap of aluminum amid a pile of rubble and ash from yards away. If Trip was working an area, I knew just to move my people along down the road, because he'd have it stripped clean of anything of value before I even got my pickings sack open.

* * *

We walked over miles of lava flows cooled and hardening into rock, a dead zone where anything of value had been permanently lost. I thought of giving karma a little nudge in the right direction, waiting till Jeff Robert and I were alone and then shooting him in the throat with one of my arrows or helping him on his way to a broken leg. Even a good sprain would be enough. We were too far from camp to deal with the injured out here. Anyone who couldn't walk back at the end of the shift would be left to die. We had just walked past the dehydrating corpse of Carl, who'd twisted his ankle last week. I sprinkled ash on his eyelids as a sign of respect, according to the new custom, and we walked through the doors of a Kohl's which, as I feared, was extremely picked over. Trip had given my team the shit assignment and I blamed Jeff Robert for this, too. My team blamed me for questioning Trip in the first place.

Now they stood in the lower level of the store, grumbling. We were looking at everything you do not want in a job. The building was still standing, but it had been so blasted by heat that the guys immediately began speculating on how long that would remain the case. Guesses ranged from a week to thirty minutes before the whole thing came down. The clothing had melted to its hangers and everything reeked of groundsmoke and was coated in ash. The footprints of other crews—many others—were visible all over the filthy floors.

"Let's get this done," I said, and led them into the dark. When our eyes adjusted we began to work, breathing through our shirts, if we had them, or rags we tied across our faces, if we had those. Jeff Robert had neither and I was pleased to see him sputter and cough as he moved through Housewears.

* * *

My pack was light—a spoon, some dirty kitchen twine, and the blade from a shattered blender—when I found the door to a tiny office just off the women's intimates section. The occupant was still at her desk, what was left of her, and my increasingly callous heart ached for this unknown woman. What a way to go.

I scooped some ash from the pile that had collected on the surface of her desktop and sprinkled it over her. Then I began to investigate the mini fridge behind her desk. A rotted clamshell of salad and protein shakes. Two of them. A sensible, filling replacement for a balanced meal. The dead woman had struggled with her weight; that's probably how she would have phrased it. She had no idea. None of us did.

A bonus of our altered circumstances, one of the very few bonuses, was that I no longer wrestled with questions of professional integrity. I put the shakes in the waistband of my pants and not in the bag without a second thought. I was bringing them to Lisa.

"Cousin," Jeff Robert said. The ponytailed piece of human garbage was standing in the doorway with a *gotcha* expression. This morning he'd stood at attention with the others as I paced the line of my crew, a little ritual before every mission, and laid out the ground rules. *Any appropriation of products reclaimed on company time will result in immediate termination.* We left it deliberately vague as to whether we meant termination from employment or from the living: that was at the discretion of the manager, but I knew what kind of mood Trip was in.

"Do we have a problem, cousin?" I said to Jeff Robert.

"No problem," Jeff Robert said. "It's just that I'm real hungry."

I passed the asshole one of my protein shakes and he cracked it open right then and there. Brazen. It was hard to watch the chocolate flavored calories pass his unworthy lips.

"I should round up the team," I said. The store's detritus was sparse and of only small value. It probably wasn't worth the damage we were doing to our lungs. We would press on to the next retail establishment.

As I moved through the door Jeff Robert's leg darted out and hit me mid-calf. I tumbled to the floor. We both heard the sick popping sound my knee made.

"My bad," Jeff Robert said, dropping his empty can into the ash.

* * *

"You okay, boss?" Enrique said, watching me limp across the cracked-up asphalt. He was my best product specialist, and he was gunning for me. The load of reclaimed products he was carrying back to camp today was, quite obviously, heavier than my own.

"Nothing serious," I said, through my teeth. The knee was swelling with every step, and I struggled to keep up with my team. We passed Carl again on the way back and—no surprise after all the groundsmoke I'd breathed in at that Kohl's—his ghost was stretched out on the lava flow, obnoxiously lounging. *We can rest when we're dead* was something I liked to say to motivate my team. Carl's ghost gave me the finger as I hobbled by.

* * *

Trip sorted through my team's haul. "Garbage, garbage, garbage—oh, *this* is nice," he said, admiring a lint roller.

We'd made quota, barely, but there would be no bonus today. Our community was situated in what had once been a city park, and Trip was something like its mayor and CEO rolled into one. The settlement abutted a major footpath, and we bartered useful items to ragged bands heading north, or sometimes, to ragged bands heading south, at an almost unconscionable mark up. Even so, nobody was getting rich.

"Any issues?" Trip said, as I hobbled up to him to receive my pay.

"Not a one," I said. I felt Jeff Robert's eyes on my back where the protein shake was hidden. Trip handed me six fresh grackle and a hot pink shoelace. Birdfall had been light today and we were on reduced rations. I didn't have the nerve to argue.

* * *

"There's no last colony. That's bull," Milo said. The three of us were sitting on a branch, spit roasting grackles over a small fire, Milo, Cerise, and me. For reasons that needed no explanation, Cerise was on Milo's boat, which was still parked in the lot of his complex, when the event began. They'd been hauling the boat down Dolorosa Street, searching for that incoming toxic sea, when they'd spotted me dragging myself up a fire escape with a serious head wound. They'd dragged me onboard the boat and then we'd picked up Lisa and the girls just a half mile away.

The last colony was a subject I often found myself raising whether at campfire or during team meetings with the product specialists who reported to me. It had come to my attention that I *harped* on it. When we convened for our Monday launch meetings at the dry fountain in the north end of the park, I tended to get off topic. I'd be giving a rundown of items that were predicted to be hot in the next period — rope, maybe, or drinking vessels — and before I could stop myself I'd be spouting off about the last colony. Looks would be exchanged like, *here we go again.* They'd keep their mouths shut till the end of the meeting, but sometimes as we moved through the dead zones, sifting through the ruins I'd hear them laughing about it among themselves.

I had every reason to harp on the last colony, more than the rest of them, even, who would be well served to wake up, take an honest inventory of our circumstances, and conclude, as I had done, that we were in a race against starvation we could not win. But there were things about myself I didn't feel like sharing. Now that my knee was swollen to twice its normal size, the colony's location felt especially pertinent.

Milo flipped his second grackle belly-side-down over the fire. He had just explained at some length, citing multiple sources in popular entertainment—a subject on which he had an encyclopedic knowledge—that the last colony was a cliché. "Of course you want to believe that there's one place where things are still up and running. We all do. But it's simply—" Milo paused to pick a feather out of his teeth, "not the case."

Milo ran food services, which meant he often had something extra to share, like the grackle I was now devouring. We'd torn through the supplies on his boat within two weeks; he only ever intended them to supplement the haul from his fishing nets. His boat was by far the most luxurious living quarters in the entire park community, and it conferred a certain status, as did his relationship with Cerise.

Cerise headed up code compliance, enforcing standards about the size and type of hovels that could be erected and the number of firearms per family. People feared her and stayed out of her way. But even though Milo was among the younger adults, it was now customary to seek his opinion before making a major decision.

"We heard it from a peddler," I said, burning my lip on the hot grackle. It tasted not unlike the meat in a Chipotle burrito, and when I'd first made that realization, another illusion of the old world was stripped away. As long as the birds held out we wouldn't starve, but they fell from the sky in such large numbers that we were sure that wouldn't be too long. Already there were off days, like this one, when most of us would go to bed hungry. Milo was trying to dry cure the birds, rubbing their bodies in salt and hanging them from a clothes line, but it was impossible to keep the flies off them and they sprouted maggots within 48 hours. He was frustrated by this and by the failure of the Gulf of Mexico. Sometimes he stood on the roof of his boat, wearing his captain's hat, with a look on his face like he was just mad at the whole world.

"Oh, well," Milo said, rolling his eyes, "if you heard it from a *peddler* than I guess it's for real." He and Cerise exchanged a look, the meaning of which pretty clearly had to do with how big of a dumbass I was. *Huge,* they agreed, though sometimes they went with *enormous.* My stupidity was just about the only thing they agreed on. They'd saved my life, but now they had zero respect for me. I'd lost my wife and children within twelve hours of the event. Without them, we'd all be dead. There were civilians who'd done better. I couldn't really take offense: I had only limited respect for myself.

Hank had called it—not only about me, but about Bat Rodney. The entire Rodney clan was indeed sitting pretty, right on top of the smoldering remains of San Antonio. They'd taken control of what was left of the city, killing on sight, and enslaving or taking prisoner whoever they found, only after they got bored of killing. The only law was the law of the gun, and so forth.

From what I knew of Bat and his family, it sounded like they were living the dream. Every day, haggard bands of escapees wandered north past Milo's boat carrying what little they had on their backs with a look in their eyes that indicated that the better part of their baggage was trauma.

"Which peddler? Was it Smokey Joe? Because I think he was mental *before* the E.O.D.," Cerise said.

Peddlers were near the bottom of the rudimentary social hierarchy that now existed. Product supply specialists like myself were not exactly the elites, but at least we ranked ahead of peddlers. *They* were ragged drifters who wandered around trading matches and other sundries for alcohol. Sometimes they simply traded in information.

"He seemed lucid," I said. I'd given Smokey Joe a warm Lone Star Light I'd found on one of my rounds through the park's shrubbery in return for the location of the colony. He'd slammed it down like the fraternity pledge he'd once been, snorting breath through his nose, and letting streams of hot foamy beer trickle into his unruly beard. Milo was angry about the wasted beer and about my gullibility, but I'd looked into Smokey Joe's eyes and found him sincere and I felt I ought to at least check his story out.

"You want to leave everything we've built here?" Milo said, gesturing toward the boat, *The Jolly Barista*, which we'd covered with branches and garbage to camouflage it from marauders. All six of us had been living in it at one time, and it hadn't seemed so bad to me at first, when I was feverish and brain-swollen, but once

I was up and around again, quarters got tight. I'd built my family a lean-to a little down the way.

"This is no place to raise children. My family deserves better," I said. And I began to cry, thinking of all the things I wanted for my kids, like flush toilets and literacy. They can't stand that, my crying. "Don't you want to find Hank, Cerise?" I sobbed.

"Well of course I do, when the time is right," Cerise said.

The quakes had been less frequent and the volcanism had been dialed down too, but it wasn't what you'd call an ideal time to set out on a hike. The truck was out of the question, even if you could refuel it. The most likely thing was you'd drive it right into a lava field and burn to death, but even if you could find enough solid ground it was too conspicuous. From what the peddlers were telling me, you could expect to be stripped clean of everything you owned, up to and including your flesh, the moment the ignition fired. "Try to look like a sad sack and you might just make it," Smokey Joe had said. The hours before my clubbing were hazy, but now a memory floated up from the depths of my splintered brain.

"You know, Hank might not be safe in the Don Cheevers," I said.

"Of course he's safe. He's actually much safer than *we* are," Cerise said, looking uneasily at the brush that surrounded us. *We* had the riders to worry about. They came around every two or three days and nobody breathed until they were gone. Today they'd come again, well-fed men on lean horses, and they hadn't left empty handed.

"Hank's got granite counters and concrete walls. I could be in a whirlpool tub right now. I guess someone made the wrong choice."

"Every night. Every night we have to do this?" Milo threw the bones of his grackle into the fire.

"Before I got hit, Andrea told me not to trust Don Cheevers."

"Who's Andrea?"

"Blaine's cokehead neighbor. They had a thing."

"Blaine and Andrea had a thing?" Milo said, taking an interest in spite of himself. Gossip was in short supply in our new situation and everyone was eager to get it. We spent our days trying to survive, and the part of our souls that followed celebrity catfights and inter-office romances died a little every day.

"No, Andrea and Don Cheevers had a thing. Andrea said she wouldn't even buy drugs from him. So she bought them from her stylist," I explained. Since the boy in the TEAM shirt had split my head open, I sometimes found it difficult to stick to the topic in question.

"The thing is, I can't sit here on this comfortable log, eating hot burritos, without a thought for the future. The birds are going to run out and we can't eat rubble and ash. If there is a last colony, the Cheevers people will know of it."

"We paid for the wine cellar upgrade on our Cheevers," Cerise said. "The bed we bought for the dog is softer than that board in *The Jolly Barista*."

Milo and I exchanged a look. Cerise still talked a lot about Cormac and we always changed the subject as quickly as possible. What with the turmoil of events on the Last Day, it seemed Hank had not had an opportunity to fill her in on the dog's whereabouts. A different kind of person might say *let bygones be bygones, what's one child-eating dog against the collapse of all of Texas?* but Cerise was not that person.

"I think Eric is right. We should go with him, Milo. If there's a last colony, we need to know that. But first we should check on Hank—he might need us." Cerise was rubbing her lower back. Milo's mattress is not ergonomic. She mentions that daily.

"Sure. Great idea. Let's do it," Milo said, but he stared into the fire like he didn't mean a word of it.

* * *

"Your roof just blew off, hippie," my father-in-law said. He was sitting on a stump, watching as the thin corrugated metal roof that was pride of our home tumbled away, leaving us with nothing but matted grass and a large stick that functioned as the beam, and piles of untraded merchandise.

"Don't get up, let me," I said, rolling my eyes. Then I chased after our roof on my injured knee as Elias sat on his ass and watched, his main occupation these days.

When the roof was reattached, Lisa and I sat together plucking the birds for dinner. A delicate peace existed between us now. I was no longer spending money we didn't have, because money wasn't even a thing. I couldn't lie to her about where I was going, because there was nowhere to go and nothing to do. And I had lost touch with Parker Saenz. I hoped she was out there somewhere, safe, but ideally not anywhere in the immediate vicinity. Lisa was beginning to trust me again. She smiled at me as she snapped the head off a grackle and I brushed her hand with mine.

"How was your day?" she asked.

"Same old, same old," I said. She was looking at my knee. "It's nothing," I said. "Honestly." Later, when it was dark, I would give her the energy drink I'd stolen her, and if she could keep it down, that would give me more pleasure than bashing Jeff Robert's skull in, which was also on my to-do list.

Isabel was crying again. "Grandpa says if we don't listen, the rednecks will eat us. I don't want to be eaten!"

"Dad!" Lisa said. She was putting the dinner birds onto the roasting sticks now, while I worked on starting the fire. Elias was supposed to be helping with the children.

"Hey, it's the truth. I don't like it any more than you do, but it's better that they know. Two big old rednecks today. They took that little bastard what's his name—the one with the crew cut who lives down by the creek?"

"Cooper," Jeanette said.

"Real disrespectful kid. He threw a rock at me day before yesterday. Anyway, we won't be seeing his smart ass around here anymore. He looks just like that right about now," Elias said, pointing to the plucked and splayed bird Jeanette was roasting on her own little stick.

"Elias, come on. We're trying to have a nice family dinner."

"Grandpa's only joking," Lisa said. But he wasn't. Milo had filled me in already.

"Do you know I arrested Bat Rodney? That was in the winter of 1979."

"We *know*," I said. If I had to sit through the story one more time, I was going to take Elias by the throat—but I stopped myself. It was one thing to think along those lines back in the old days, when you knew you'd never really do it, and a totally different thing to think that way now, when there was absolutely nothing to stop you. But Elias was doing it; he was telling the story again.

"Bar fight. Man, if I'd busted his head when I had the chance. Make it look like it was from the fight, you know? Easiest thing in the world. I could have saved us all a lot of damn trouble. I blame myself, tell you the truth."

"It's not your fault, Dad," Lisa said.

"Have mine, too. I ate at Milo's," I said, passing Lisa my bird. There was hardly any meat on them, and I could easily have eaten five or six more, but I pretended not to be hungry. Even Jeanette and Isabel could handle two each, but Lisa was eating almost nothing. She held the gray slightly charred bird flesh but she didn't take a bite. Even the smell made her sick.

"You don't want it, pass it over," Elias said, and he ripped into it, smacking and crunching right through the smaller bones. The older generation was having trouble adjusting to subsistence living. They clung to the old ways, complained constantly about the lack of air conditioning and running water, ate everything in sight, and generally failed to pull their weight. Many seniors had been driven out of their families to save resources, and so it brought us great status, having an elder in the household, especially one as ostentatiously idle as Elias. The old man's presence around our fire impressed the others, the way flashing a Rolex or owning a vacation home would have only a few months before. But sometimes as I watched him wrap his lips around a third or even a *fourth* grackle at the dinner rock, it was all I could do not to knock him off his comfortable stump and drive him from our lean-to into the dark.

"I tell you what," Elias said, picking the bones cleans. "One of those honky-tonk pieces of shit catches you, you bash your head against a rock first chance you get. You remember what your Grandpa told you, girls. There's dying and then there's *dying*. You don't want to do it the second way."

* * *

I passed Lisa the protein shake in the dark and the sound it made when she opened it almost brought me to tears. I cried a lot, yes, but there was no shame in it these days. The pop of an aluminum can, a garbage truck beeping in reverse, the whine of a television—I missed these noises as much as I hated the sound of horse hooves, the shrieks of dying birds, and the rumble of buildings falling in on themselves.

"Do you like it?" I whispered. She said she did, but I couldn't see her face. When she kissed me goodnight I tasted its chalky artificial cocoa flavor, the slight tang of aluminum. It was so sweet and delicious, and knowing that Jeff Robert had also tasted that, a whole can of it, made up my mind.

* * *

Elias was supposed to be doing the first watch, but as usual, he wasn't taking it seriously. His snoring woke me only ten minutes into his shift. "The bastards hunt in the daytime. There's no point," he said when I shook him awake, but I explained that wasn't the reason I'd interfered with his rest.

"Jeff Robert that married my cousin Evelyn's girl?" Elias said. "You wake me up at—what time is it, like 9:30 in the night—" We all went to bed early these days, sans electricity. "You wake me up at 9:30 to kill *him*? Can't it wait?"

I explained that it could not. Marissa's ghost was standing, cross armed and impatient, at the door of our lean-to, but I didn't mention that to Elias. We walked quietly through the dark, following Marissa past our sleeping fellow residents.

"I'm too old for this," Elias said. "All of this. I tell you, I wish it had happened sooner. This had gone down in the 80s no way I'd be sleeping on the ground, begging for my supper. I would have been running things. Guys like me, we were made for this stuff. But I just never got this kind of opportunity," Elias said. He was actually wistful.

* * *

Jeff Robert was bad off. He had one of the worst sleeping spots in the entire community, being alone, being a newcomer. He had no soft grass and not a scrap of shelter; he was snoring heavily on a stretch of bare, rocky ground, and fire ants traveled over the exposed flesh of his arms.

"Okay, let's get this done and go back to bed." Elias bent over Jeff Robert, studying him. "There's the spot you want," he said pointing to his temple. "Quick and clean. No time for screaming. Count of three. One... two..." I raised the rock. "Three," Elias said.

I was bringing the rock down on Jeff Robert's temple when Marissa's scream ripped my eardrums to shreds; it was a sound only I could hear. The rock was already arcing toward him. I swiveled and brought it down hard on his shoulder. Jeff Robert woke with a scream that was audible to everyone, and Elias and I ran for it.

* * *

"You lost your nerve, hippie. Now we've got problems."

"I didn't lose my nerve," I said. "He had his kid with him." That's what Marissa had seen at the last minute. The boy, Louis, was sleeping beside him.

"So what if he had his kid? Not our problem," Elias said. "You know what makes me laugh? Back when people like you were running things, *this* was all you could think about, the way the world was going to be after. Now it's here and you're terrible at it. Just terrible."

"I'm a team leader," I said.

"Congratulations. You're the number one garbage picker," Elias said. I was number two, actually, but I didn't point that out.

* * *

"You know what's funny? I'm not even mad," Trip said. He held the empty aluminum can in his hand and stared at it like it was a mysterious object from a lost world, which it was. "I guess what I am, is disappointed."

I'd planned to take the can with me to work that day and drop it in some convenient out-of-the-way spot when nobody was around to see. But HR had come at first light, and they'd searched our lean-to before I'd had a chance to dispose of the evidence. They were acting on an "anonymous tip." Now they stood outside our door, with their guns pointed more or less in my direction, while Trip Edmonds fired me for the second time.

Jeff Robert was among the group of onlookers who'd gathered to witness my downfall and I was pleased to see that his shoulder looked even worse than my knee. Murder, attempted or completed, was viewed as a private matter, so long as it happened after hours and was carried out with personal property. But misappropriation of resources was the unforgiveable sin, and with that slim aluminum can, Jeff Robert had sealed my fate.

Still, I tried. I fell to my knees and begged for my job. I explained our situation. I appealed to their compassion, but even Elias was unmoved.

"What? What the hell is the matter with you?" Elias said. "There's no room in this place for a baby. Crying all the damn time, keeping everybody up. And what about diapers? You want to use some leaves for that? *Stupid* idea.I should have busted *your* head when I had the chance," Elias said.

In fact, the baby was a terrible idea, and I'd thought so from the moment Lisa looped me in on the situation. But obviously this was nobody's *idea.* I've tried to imagine breaking that to this future son or daughter, if both it and I live long enough for it to have questions about why Lisa and I brought it into this world. I will have to put an arm around the kid's shoulders and say, "Son or daughter, you were an oversight at a time of great upheaval that, unfortunately, coincided with a rare moment of marital détente." That's a lot to lay on a kid, especially one who has never experienced the simple joys of tap water and refrigeration.

Jeanette and Isabel will grow up dirty, ignorant, and underfed, and comfortable in a society in which cannibalism has replaced low carb diets, but at least they will retain some hazy early memories of a world that more or less worked. Whereas *this kid* is completely screwed. Of all my many mistakes as a husband and father, I considered the third child to be the most egregious.

"Yeah, that's just not going to cut it," Trip Edmonds said. I didn't much care for the look he was giving Lisa. She hadn't said a word from the moment HR ripped off our metal roof and began to tear up our home.

"What about him," I said, pointing at Jeff Robert, who was loitering at the edge of the crowd. "He's as guilty as I am. More so. He took a can for himself and didn't report it. I *saw him* drink it."

HR waved Jeff Robert over. The crowd parted for him and he begged for his life. I'd led him astray. I'd told him the rules didn't apply to supervisors or their kin. The crowd grumbled At night people sat around their campfires and claimed management kept all the best things for themselves.

"I assure you, that couldn't be further from the truth," Trip said, holding up his hands and calling for order. "The rules are the rules."

"Eric said it was kind of a wink-wink, nod-nod policy and I should pay no attention to it. He said you and he kicked back with your secret supply of foodstuffs on the regular," Jeff Robert said.

This was patently ridiculous, in Trip's case, but though I had dropped a shocking amount of weight, I was still looking pretty robust by the standards of the day. Many of the onlookers hadn't known me *before*, and I could see they were suspicious. I was hearty and strong. I sported a very becoming BMI, and I had been caught with a stolen can—what more did they need to know? The crowd looked like it wanted to hang Trip Edmonds by his electrical cord belt and beat me to death with the pole of my own lean-to.

Trip assessed the crowd's mood and made a tough call. "I'm afraid that you were badly misled by this man, Jeff Robert. We can't hold you responsible, sir. It was your first day on the job. The blame lies here," Trip said, pointing at me. "And I think it lies with no one else. Let's not make this into a witch hunt," Trip said, now addressing himself directly to Jeff Robert.

Jeff Robert nodded; he was willing to play ball. He pointed at me, too, and raised his voice for the crowd. "This man was my insurance agent. This man was my family. Peace of mind is what he promised me." Jeff Robert slowly peeled off his bloody shirt and displayed his injuries. "But this is what he gave me instead."

The crowd was now whipped up into a frenzy of anti-Eric sentiment. "Kill him!" a woman screamed. Her name was Kim and she had been a cashier at the lawn and garden big box near our home. We'd once been on friendly terms, once. A few others expressed their preference for my immediate demise; a sort of chant was being taken up. HR pointed their guns at the crowd to quell it.

"*People*. We have policies in place for this kind of thing. Let's not be led by emotions," Trip said.

"I'll resign if that's what you want," I said to Trip.

"I think that's for the best. And I'll need you to sign this non-compete clause," Trip said, scrawling some legalese in the dirt with a stick.

"But that's a death sentence," I said. The dirt letters spelled out my promise that I wouldn't scavenge for items either useable or edible anywhere within the territory formerly known as Texas for the next five years.

"Your other option is literally a death sentence," Trip said. The big guns from HR nodded their agreement.

I took the stick from Trip and made my mark in the dirt.

* * *

"Well now what?" Lisa said, when the onlookers drifted away.

"First I'm going to kill Jeff Robert, and then I'm going to find the Don Cheevers with Milo and Cerise."

If Marissa's ghost had a problem with that, well then *too bad*. I'd do my best to make sure that Louis wasn't around to witness his father take a boulder in the brains, but she wasn't entirely up to speed on what a brutal place the world had become. Her qualms were impossibly quaint and fussy things now, like grapefruit spoons or finger bowls.

"You are not going to *kill* Jeff Robert," Lisa said. "I was a bridesmaid in his wedding."

I tried to reason with Lisa—after all, Jeff Robert's teary vows and sentimental first dance hadn't precluded *him* from doing a little killing—but she was adamant. So I scrapped the boulder plans and said my goodbyes.

"Just make sure she eats," I said to Elias.

"Eats *what*?" I was leaving them in a terrible position. Elias was too old for product reclamation; he thought he might hang out his shingle as violence coach, but so much violence among the chronically malnourished was a spontaneous affair, and demand for planned revenge or score-settling was uncertain. He and Lisa and the girls would have to scrounge grackles outside the safety of the park or earn their food fetching water for better-off families.

* * *

It just about killed Milo to leave his boat and in fact he would not agree to do it until we had heaped another layer of greenery and debris over it. Cerise promised that the two of them would be back before nightfall, and Milo made her hold up her hand and swear it. He made each of them strap on a life jacket, too. "Some people don't know when to quit," Cerise said, as Milo held out the orange life vest for her to take.

"I have two conditions, and this is one of them," Milo said. Cerise began to strap the thing on.

"What's the other condition?" I said, but they both looked at me like *butt out*. I was obviously going to be the third wheel on this trip.

* * *

"I just hate leaving a thing half done," I said, as Milo, Cerise, and I stepped out onto the open road.

"What are you talking about?" Cerise said.

"Jeff Robert," I said.

Milo gave me a look like *drop it.* I'd wanted him to do it for me, and in exchange, I'd promised to kill Hank at the first opportunity, but Milo had balked. "That's not necessary. I think the stress is getting to you, Eric," he'd said. I'd accused him of going soft, of inhabiting a pre-doomsday mentality that had no place in our current circumstances. Hank would have told him the same thing. Kill or be killed: if he'd said it once, he'd said it a thousand times. Milo was letting his guilt over the affair cloud his judgment. When Hank came for him, and he would, it would be cold comfort that Milo had spent many tender moments with his wife. On that day, Milo would exchange even his best moments with Cerise for a second chance to put a pastry wheel in that guy's chest. I'd explained all this to Milo.

"Just let me shoot him on sight, because when you show up with his wife, it's going to be clear you're cheating on him," I whispered.

"I'm not *cheating* on Hank. I'm Sancho-ing him," Milo said. "And no, thank you."

"Either way," I said, "you will live to regret your sentimentality." Of that, I was certain.

As we left the community and started out on the open road, I looked back and saw Trip Edmonds hunkered down amid the mesquite brush, desperately trying to lick some drops from the bottom of the stolen can.

* * *

To the best of Cerise's recollection, the site of the Don Cheevers was a little more than three miles from where *The Jolly Barista* was moored. We'd go there, and then with help from Hank and whoever else was in residence, we'd press on to the last colony. The plan was ridiculous on its face, but nobody wanted to hear the facts of the matter, which were that Hank wouldn't have helped me during the golden age of civilization, let alone now, and that he was unlikely to welcome Milo with open arms, given that Cerise had been welcoming Milo with open arms behind Hank's back. I'd advocated for skipping Hank and just going right to the location Smokey Joe had described, but I'd been outvoted.

"First of all it doesn't exist. But if it does exist, it's probably some kind of a trap. We need intel before we just waltz into the unknown," Milo had said.

So we were headed to the Cheevers now, using what remained of the Tower of the Americas as our point of reference. The base of the tower still stood, though its top was missing. It looked like a dandelion somebody had blown the head off.

We'd gone maybe a mile in the right direction—or as Milo kept saying to Cerise, *what you think is the right direction*—when we hit our first setback. We walked through the remnants of a gated community where all the streets were named some kind of bluff, *Bluff View, North Bluff, Hunter's Bluff,* when a man on a bony horse came riding slowly out of the cul de sac on Bluff View Circle. His beard reached halfway down his filthy t-shirt which said Programmers Do It In Code. He was well-fed and strong, yet he had the look of hunger, too. The horse walked with its head drooped. I didn't even wait for the vote. I hit him in the forearm with an arrow, and he fell out of the saddle and into the street. The horse stood there, moving it dry lips over its big long teeth.

"Wow, Eric. A little hasty, don't you think?"

"I don't remember voting on that," Cerise said as we watched the stranger's death throes.

I was on the wrong side of the law, cast out from the community, and suddenly I was comfortable just calling them as I saw them. For the first time in my life I didn't have a supervisor to answer to. I was my own boss, and it was exhilarating.

"I just don't trust someone that well-fed on a horse that skinny. He's obviously not on the grackle diet," I said. He'd been riding in the direction of the park, but I didn't say that out loud. I removed my arrow from his arm and tried not to think about it. I had to hope that Lisa could take care of herself and the girls, and Elias had already lived a full life, so there was no point in fretting. We stepped over the rider and let the horse wander off down the empty streets of the subdivision.

We walked through the deserted suburbs and strip malls, and when we reached the handicapped spaces of The Barbecue Station we came to a lava field that stretched out in all directions. The land near the edge of the lava had a springy, uncertain feel, as if it might cleave off from the rest of the crust and drift. There were bits of asphalt and topsoil floating across the molten surface which told me I was right to worry.

I had another reason to worry, but it was kind of embarrassing to bring up, so I said nothing. We walked a long way and when we were nearly at the far end of the lake, a small fissure at lake's edge blew up a wisp of groundsmoke and the three of us walked right through it. I gritted my teeth and kept my eyes on my feet. We'd barely finished coughing when it started.

"Excuse me!"

I recognized the voice, of course. My head snapped up before I could stop it. A man was bobbing in the middle of the fire lake, speaking on an old style telephone with a cord. Once you've made eye contact, it's all over. You just have to play along until the breeze picks up or it will not go well for you. Earlier in the week, I was extracting a vacuum cleaner tube from under a brick pile when a 17th century Spanish missionary had popped up from the ground and sunk his teeth into my ankle, all because I made some abrupt Spanglish excuses and tried to exit his rambling Castilian conversation before he was ready to end it.

"Are you the one who makes the pants?" the man in the lake yelled into his phone.

"No sir," I said, quietly. I didn't have the nerve to ignore him.

"Well find out who made these up and let them know they're a little too tight in the crotch. They cut me. It's just like riding a wire fence. I want you to give me just as much room as you can down there." A piece of earth floated toward him and he swatted it out of the way.

"Okay," I said.

"I want them the color of a lady's face powder. And make the pockets bigger by an inch. When I sit down my knife and my money fall out."

"Yes, sir," I said. "Where should I have them sent?"

"White House."

"Are you *talking to someone* Eric?" Cerise said. I pointed to the large jowly man in the lake, who was bigger than in life, so big he was out of scale. The hand that held the telephone could have encircled my head.

"You're talking to the lava?" She was hot and irritated. She'd snapped at Milo for humming a minute ago and I didn't have the nerve to tell her the truth.

"Just thinking out loud," I said as LBJ sank below the surface of the lake.

* * *

It had taken, Milo pointed out, more than double the time Cerise had anticipated, and we were still not at the site of the Don Cheevers. Nor had we seen a single other (live) person since the well-fed coder, a fact I found increasingly unnerving. The body of an EPA agent hung from an overpass, covered with grackles, and the scent of death leaked out from piles of roadside rubble, making us wretch. I kept my crossbow slung over my shoulder, but Milo wouldn't let me load an arrow onto it. I was getting pretty sick of being treated like a prisoner.

Many of the houses had collapsed in on themselves during the quakes and the streets were lined with the carcasses of rotting birds. Some do-gooder had put up a sign that read DANGER TURN BACK but we ignored it. The danger was everywhere and there was no back to turn to, but it was hard to keep our minds on it. We were getting thirsty. Our throats burned with the smoky air, and the water Cerise clearly remembered putting in her pack was not there.

"If you're going to accuse me of something, then just accuse me," Milo said.

"I didn't say a word," Cerise said. She was carrying two loaded shotguns and Milo had some sort of antique pistol on his hip. The mood was tense as we trudged through one abandoned neighborhood after the next, until we passed the shell of a Panera and Cerise stopped and said, "It should be right here." But there was nothing in sight.

"Unless this is the wrong Panera," I said.

"Exactly. Would it have killed you to use a local bakery as your landmark?" Milo said.

"I like Panera," Cerise said. "The prices are reasonable and the quality is consistent."

I winced on Milo's behalf. She knew just how to hurt him. "What are you going to do when you get there, Cerise?"

"Take a bath," Cerise said.

"You know what I mean. What will you say to him?" Milo had stopped walking. He removed his enormous, soot-streaked glasses and began to clean them with the hem of his shirt. I wondered what *I* would say to Hank, but I knew if I mentioned that the meeting would be awkward for me, too, the two of them would accuse me of always having to make everything about myself.

"Milo, you are a pain in the ass. You are *almost* as big a pain in the ass as Eric."

"Hey!" I said.

"I feel betrayed," Milo said.

"You feel betrayed. Listen to yourself, Milo. *You* feel betrayed. Hank was your friend."

"He still is my friend. That's why you have to say something."

"It's not the right time," Cerise said. She gestured to the empty, rubble strewn streets, the piles of dead birds, the ashy sky. Milo shook his head.

"You always say that. I don't think it's honest. I'm beginning to think that you're not serious about me."

Cerise lowered her shotguns and pressed the muzzles into Milo's chest. "You are twenty-five years old. *Of course* I'm not serious about you!" The mission was devolving fast.

"Look!" I whispered. Ahead of us was the geodesic dome of Living Waters church. The front door was open and inside, somebody was playing the organ.

* * *

Milo put his finger over his lips and the three of us stepped through the doors of the church silently. We pointed our weapons at the organist, but she turned around, very nonchalant, before Milo, who had insisted upon being the one to speak for the three of us, could come up with anything to say. A certain type of person might seem all the more threatening for pointing a gun silently, without making any demands, but Milo couldn't quite pull it off. He was wearing jodphurs and a life vest.

The organist, a small unarmed woman in her 60s, looked at the three of us and was obviously thinking *amateur hour*. "What can I get you?" she said. She was clean and she wore an animal print blouse with ruffles and a pair of yoga pants and compared to the three of us, she was dazzling. My clothes were filthy and blood crusted, and despite all the birds I'd eaten, my pants were beginning to sag. Cerise and Milo were somewhat better off— Cerise in a sundress and ropers, Milo in the jodphurs and plaid, but their hygiene was not what it once was. Cerise had said that Milo looked like a pirate called Debris Beard.

"We're thirsty," I blurted out.

The woman laughed a chesty smoker's cackle. "Is that all? Go get yourselves a seat."

* * *

The woman served us beer in cans, which we drank too fast, due to the dehydration. She brought out more as soon as we finished. She did the same again when we drank down the second cans, and as we sipped our third, Milo began to recount an episode of *Moonshine Ranch* scene by scene. Cerise rolled her eyes. This was a liability of hanging out with Milo when alcohol was involved. But our host seemed to enjoy it.

It still made me nervous to be in buildings; they were just rubble that hadn't happened yet. But I looked around and tried to make sense of the place. Living Waters was kind of low on decorations. There was a bright blue carpet throughout and a Jacuzzi bubbling at the front, which looked so inviting that I'd agreed to be baptized as soon as we finished this round. But it was anybody's guess what sort of gods were worshiped here, because they were nowhere represented along the carpeted walls.

We finished the beers and our host, who we now knew was the Rev. Tif Buckle, dunked us one by one in the warm bubbling water. Then we sat dripping in the front pew and Milo started in on episode 39, *My Friend, My Enemy*. We made some excuse to be on our way, which was harder to do than it used to be. There were no jobs or appointments, no handy reason why we couldn't sit here under the dome talking about television programs of the late 1960s indefinitely.

"You can't leave yet," the Rev. Buckle said. She requested just one more, the episode where the youngest of the brothers, Chick Cooper, tried his luck with the mentally unstable daughter of an area rancher and nearly brought the law down on everyone's heads.

"Oh, *A Woman Scorned?* That one is a classic. Excellent choice," Milo said.

"Hold on just a minute. Let me get the rest of the gang," our host said and she disappeared through a door in the back.

"Let's run for it," I said. The three of us sprinted for the exit.

"What's your hurry, boys?" our host yelled, and we froze. Two enormous men in braids had joined her. They wore bandoliers across their chest, Pancho Villa style, and once they had probably driven trucks with frightening bumper stickers.

"No hurry," Milo said. "We just didn't want to overstay our welcome."

"Impossible," the largest and scariest of the men said. "You've found your church home. All are welcome in the house of the Lord." But in spite of these friendly words, they looked at me like the Lord might have his limits.

* * *

The terrifying giants were the Rev. Buckle's twin sons, Rolph and Craig, both Elders in the church. They'd all been prepping for years, studying the Maya texts and gearing up for the 2012 event, but when that didn't happen they'd kept the faith. Every Sunday they'd passed the plate and each and every cent collected was put toward laying in supplies for these times. The community was extremely well outfitted, a hundred and fifty strong, all living in a shelter below the church. The way they saw it, we'd agreed to join them. By accepting their beer and the baptisms, we'd declared our intention to stay with them in these last days, until whatever deity or deities they subscribed to showed up and finished us all off. It seemed late in the day to ask for the details of their belief system, so we just played along.

"We'd love to stay," Cerise said, smiling at the slightly more enormous twin, Craig, who had taken a strong liking to her. He'd let her know he was "down a wife," and he was stroking her damp hair with his big pale hand. Milo looked like he was working up his nerve to politely object to this. "But unfortunately we have obligations out there."

Rev. Buckle wasn't happy, but she said we were free to go as soon as we paid for our drinks. Nobody took money anymore, of course, but every last thing we offered them was refused. In fairness, we didn't have much worth taking—shoelaces, matches, some breath mints. They agreed to take our life jackets for one round, but that left two still to pay for. Finally we offered our weapons. They sneered at my crossbow and poison arrows. They briefly considered taking Cerise's shotguns, "for the kids," but decided the kick would be too much for the little ones and anybody over age nine would be ashamed of such weapons. Milo's derringer pistol took black powder and when that was discovered, it made him an instant laughing stock. "This guy— he's too much," the Rev. Buckle said, wiping tears from her eyes.

"Why don't we keep him?" Elder Rolph said. Unfortunately for Milo, the idea caught on. A defector had absconded with the bulk of the community's DVD collection and they were low on entertainment. They could spend the last days around the fire pit, listening to Milo recount every episode of *Moonshine Ranch.*

"Okay. Shake on it," Cerise said, and she and Rev. Buckle sealed the deal.

"We can't just leave Milo," I said as I followed Cerise to the door. Milo watched Cerise walk up the aisle to the exit, like a bride in reverse, looking like his heart would break. "Cerise, it's not right," I said.

"We have no choice," Cerise said. She was not a sentimental woman.

"Hold up! We ought to keep that one, too," one of the Elders said, "*the big one.*" Cerise and I froze, but obviously they meant me. Cerise ran for the door and the Elders took me by the arms. I heard the report of a 19th century pistol and Rev. Buckle fell head first into her baptismal Jacuzzi, spurting blood. Milo dropped the gun. The derringer could get off only one shot every half hour or so, and it had burned his fingers.

"That one's mine," Parker Saenz said. She'd appeared on the altar platform—and where she'd appeared from I could not have said—and she was holding my crossbow, but casually, as if she had nothing to fear from the Elders. The sight of her moved me, as it always did. She was so tiny and beautiful and terrifying. "Hands off."

"He killed Mama!" Elder Craig screamed.

"I have claimed him and I have written my claim in the Book of Counsel and sealed it with the sign of Seven Macaw," Parker said, as if explaining something to an obtuse reservations agent or customer service rep.

Whatever it meant, it was air tight. Craig and Rolph conferred, and I could see by the look on their faces that they wanted to object, but there just wasn't any easy comeback to it. The Rev. Buckle's legs were still twitching and as I watched, the bubbling water turned slowly red.

"But we've got a blood debt on our hands now," Elder Rolph said, letting go of my arm. The three of them began to argue in a language I didn't catch a word of, but it was clear by their expressions that things were getting heated. Parker had put down my crossbow to free up her hands for making big emphatic gestures, and I took a few steps toward it. Nobody seemed to notice.

"Just remember this conversation the next time I ask you for a favor," Rolph said.

"Oh, certainly," Parker said. I fired a poisoned arrow into Rolph's stomach. He was still doing a slo-mo stagger toward the carpet when I shot another at Craig. They fell almost in unison. The two big men convulsed on the church floor, spitting foam and tearing at their skin. I took a certain satisfaction in it, but Parker was staring at me as if she weren't sure what to think.

I shrugged. *Sorry.*

"Don't forget your arrows," she said, after a minute.

I carefully pulled the arrows from the guts of Craig and Rolph and ran out of the church after Cerise and Milo.

* * *

"So *that's* your church?" I said to Parker as we walked along the cracked-up highway toward the Don Cheevers. I wanted to clear the air. Nobody had said a word in a long time. Cerise kept looking over her shoulder for whoever might be coming after us. Milo stumbled along; he had just killed for the first time and he'd also been traded for beer by his married older girlfriend, and he was having trouble processing these two disparate but equally upsetting experiences. I had never killed before today either, not counting Cormac, but in the course of my professional life I'd often wanted to, and I was a little disturbed by how easily it came to me.

"Since I was a little girl," Parker said, cheerfully. She smiled as if she were remembering pot luck suppers and youth group sing-alongs and other innocent pastimes.

"Okay," I said, thinking of the two poisoned giants and their reverend mother. Nothing about her attitude indicated that she particularly minded what I'd done back there, even though she seemed to be on pretty cozy terms with the three corpses we'd left behind.

"Okay," I said. We were all dealing with things in our own way.

* * *

"It's right around here," Cerise said. "It's only like three blocks from the Panera." We were standing in the middle of a field. "Hank!" she yelled.

I waited for a tree stump to flip up like a door on a hinge. Maybe Hank would pop out like a curious prairie dog and sniff the wind. But nothing happened. A flock of birds spiraled over us, dropping a few fresh ones at our feet.

"Who's hungry?" Milo said. Everyone was. I started a fire and Milo scooped up an armload of freshly dead grackle.

"We will not eat of the flesh of birds," Parker said.

Milo stood staring at Parker like she was a little nuts, which she clearly was. I'd been waiting for an opportunity to warn him about that. While Milo and Cerise had walked ahead, arguing between themselves, I'd asked where she was headed and how long she planned to stay with us, and I had not gotten a straight answer. "Till the great wheel of time breaks its spokes," she said, with a lunatic, but very lovely, smile. That sounded pretty short-term, though, so I didn't worry too much. We'd had many painful conversations about how "us" could never happen but that was all *before*, and it had been somewhat easier to stick to my guns when she wasn't constantly draped around me like a poncho.

Now Milo looked from Cerise to me, waiting for somebody to back him up, to tell Parker we most certainly *did* eat of the flesh of birds, but nobody would meet his eyes. Cerise was a little afraid of Parker, and I was too busy being nonchalant. Parker was stroking my head the way one might a friendly house cat's. This head-petting thing was just a little platonic affection between two friends; I was cool with it, or so I hope it seemed to everyone else.

Not getting any backup for his first reaction, Milo decided to play it differently. "I understand where you're coming from. I was lacto-ovo before all this. But, you know, desperate times." Milo began to impale the birds on sticks for roasting. "Plus, they'll just go to waste."

"None for me," I said.

"None for *you?*" Milo said. Even Cerise, who had been studying the toes of her boots for the past quarter of an hour looked up. It was the first time I'd refused food of any sort since before I began my famine prep program, more than a year ago.

Cerise and Milo began to pluck the feathers from their birds. "You know what makes me sad?" Milo said, working a tough one out from the lower wing. The three of us stared at him. "When a friend gets into a new relationship and totally changes who he is. That makes me sad."

This was unfair. It was possible, likely even, that certain aspects of my personality had shifted and changed as our world unraveled, but my relationship with Parker—if that's what it was—was not the cause, but a symptom. No way would I be this fireside cozy with an admin if our governor were back in Austin with his boots on his desk, running things. Only this afternoon Milo had shot a priestess in the head, but I didn't blame *Cerise* for that. I blamed the times.

"I haven't changed any more than is necessary," I said. Despite what it looked like at the moment, my goals remained constant. I scooted away from Parker and looked Milo right in the eye. "Finding the last colony and reuniting with my family remains my top priority."

"Then take a bird, my friend," Milo said, passing me a stick. "I plucked it for you and everything."

"Don't," Parker said. She was getting drowsy, and resting her head on my shoulder. I couldn't fathom how her hair could smell so good in circumstances like these. It was unnatural.

"No thanks," I said.

Milo shook his head and put his bird over the fire. There was smoke from the fire, certainly, and whether there was groundsmoke mingling in with it from some fissure we hadn't noticed, nobody could have said. But as soon as the birds began to sizzle on their sticks, they also began to caw and flap their wings. Cerise dropped hers into the fire immediately, but Milo held on to the stick for a moment, watching as the bird craned its featherless head to peck his hands, before he let it go. There was an awkward silence as we watched the birds burn down into bone and ash. I had the feeling that words would soon be exchanged. Somehow, they blamed me for this.

Milo sat down on a rock near the fire and steepled his hands, looking up to the stars that burned through the ashy sky for strength. "Look, I'll be the one to say it if nobody else will. Your girlfriend there? She's a sorceress. Wake up and smell the coffee, Eric."

Parker had fallen asleep with her head in my lap. "She's not my girlfriend," I whispered.

"But you admit she's a sorceress," Milo said.

"No way. She was an administrative assistant," I said.

"Sure, maybe she was. We were all something else. I was an artisan baker and now I am a captain without a ship. But let me ask you this. How many times have we eaten bird?"

"Three times a day, from the get-go," I admitted.

"And that has never happened before," Cerise said.

"Maybe those were *too* fresh," I said. "Let's try again with some that have been in the dirt a little longer."

"Wow," Milo said. "Just wow. You read about relationships like this. But you of all people."

I wasn't sure what he meant by that, *me of all people*, but I was pretty sure from the way she looked at me that Cerise would have liked to point a shotgun my direction and be rid of me, but for the alleged sorceress sleeping in my lap. Anyway, we skipped dinner that night.

* * *

In the morning Parker Saenz was gone, and I was back to being the third wheel.

"Oh, that's rough. *Ouch*," Milo said, when he found me sleeping with my face nuzzled against the bare dirt instead of Parker. "But I'm sure she'll call." Then he and Cerise laughed unpleasantly.

"You've got the wrong idea. It's not like that between us," I said, brushing dirt from my cheek. "She's more of a spirit guide."

"Sure. That's what it looked like," Milo said. He and Cerise were already walking in the direction of downtown, a bold move, because word on the peddler circuit was that the entire area was Bat Rodney's territory. But the Panera Cerise had taken as her landmark yesterday had evidently been the wrong Panera. There was another one, just south of downtown, and *that* Panera was the one that was near the Cheevers.

* * *

We were sitting in the rubble filled lobby of the Crockett Hotel, drinking hot Big Reds and eating barbecue chips from a vending machine that remained miraculously uncrushed. Food was somewhat more plentiful here, but other goods were in short supply. A tavern keeper named Skinny Liz controlled the machine's stock and we'd traded my brown wool dress socks for the drinks and news of any kind.

Liz had my socks tucked into her belt and I looked at them with regret. I was worried about blisters and about how it would look to wear oxfords with bare ankles, but Skinny Liz was a notch or two above the peddling class, and she only accepted luxury items, such as intimates and accessories.

Cerise had refused to hand over her bra, and Milo was in sandals, and the two of them stared at me so long that it began to get uncomfortable. In the end I felt obligated to peel off the socks and hand them over.

"You got some bad information. There never was a Panera this far south. And the Rodneys are not that big of a factor. Most of them were home schooled and they're not all that comfortable outside the compound," Liz said. We were speaking in hushed voiced because there were regular patrols around here.

"Hey, *I* was home schooled," Milo said, "and I am *very* well adjusted."

"The grownups are talking, sweetie," Cerise said, putting her fingers over his lips.

"Where are you all from, anyway?" Skinny Liz said. You could tell at a glance we weren't city folk. Most of the residents of the city center wore novelty Texas t-shirts, boots, and velvet sombreros, items scavenged from the remains of Market Square. Liz had on a tie-dyed t-shirt that said TEQUILA and she wore a midnight blue sombrero cinched tight under her chin. It sparkled with faux gems.

"We live in the old park, up by the northern lava wastes. You know, near the Captain Burger sign," I said.

"Don't think I know it. Who's your leader?"

"Trip Edmonds," I said.

"Oh, wow. Trip Edmonds, the farmer?" Liz had been a little condescending to us till now, as we were a bunch of dirty, rag-wearing bumpkins, but this impressed her.

"He's no farmer," I said. The idea of Trip Edmonds tilling the earth was comical, even back in the days when the earth cooperated in such enterprises. I had been somewhat fussy about my appearance, but *Trip* had had a punch card at Alamo Tan and a standing Thursday pedicure.

"Trip's in product reclamation. We service the north/south footpath," I said, with stupid pride, momentarily forgetting my termination.

"Yeah, so that's the story, huh?" Liz said. "But he's definitely a farmer. I see his crops heading to Alamo Plaza every few days. He supplies the new guy."

"Supplies him with what?" I said. Nothing grew beneath the shadow of the Captain Burger sign but weeds and mesquite brush.

"Meat," Liz said. "You never noticed?"

I was beginning to have doubts about Liz's brain function. "Farmers grow stuff—*did* grow stuff. Corn, soy, what have you. Meat is supplied by ranchers." I looked over at Milo and Cerise, hoping to be confirmed in this opinion, but the two of them looked stricken.

"The riders, stupid. Eric, what she's telling us is that Trip is selling *us* to the riders," Cerise said.

"That's right," Liz said, bobbing her sombrero in a nod. The look Trip had given Lisa at my termination proceedings came back to me now. It was a cold, appraising look. It was the kind of look I had many times given to a cellophane wrapped side of beef under the fluorescent lights of a grocery store, while I pushed my cart through the aisles and calming instrumental jazz leaked from the speakers. I began to scream, and Liz stuffed my socks in my mouth to silence me.

* * *

Liz believed that the Panera Cerise remembered had actually been a bagel franchise. It was no longer standing, but she agreed to walk us in the right direction. I wanted to go back for Lisa immediately but Cerise said it was suicide, and so she would have no problem shooting me if I even attempted to return before she and Milo were ready to go with me. My fellow residents had been on the point of killing me only a short time ago and it was unlikely absence had made their hearts grow fonder. Milo argued the situation required stealth and subtlety, not me rushing into camp and screaming unpalatable truths nobody would want to hear. "You go running back there now, and the most likely thing is Trip will hand you all over to the riders immediately. Let's get Hank's help on this. Be big enough to admit you need it, Eric," Milo said.

"So who's running things down here?" Cerise said.

"New guy. Real asshole," Liz said.

"Anyone we'd know?" Milo said.

"Doubt it. He didn't prep."

The three of us stared at her. "He *didn't prep*?" I said.

"Is he convulsing?" Liz asked, pointing at Milo.

"That's just how he laughs," I said. I didn't see anything funny about it, but Milo was spitting Big Red from his canteen all over his beard.

"HE DIDN'T PREP!" Milo screamed. "And now he's running the city!"

"Keep it down," Liz said, scanning the empty street. "I need you to get him under control," she said to Cerise.

"That's *enough*," Cerise said, and Milo pulled it together.

"I can't believe this. Look at our group. There's *me*." My failure to rise to the top of the new order was self-evident, even to Liz, whom I'd just met, so I didn't feel the need to elaborate. "Then there's you two, with a boat in the middle of a city park."

"Oh, that *is* dumb," Liz said.

"The sea levels are rising *as we sit here*," Milo said, getting defensive.

"Lorna and Doug?"

"Earthquake," Cerise said. I ticked off the other members of the Alamo Preppers and Cerise filled me in on their fates: Martin, Jolene, the Urbans, Ted and Julio, the Espiñoza-Taylors, each and every one of them had been killed in the first week. It was as Cerise said, a piss-poor showing. "The only one maybe doing okay is Hank," she concluded. "He should have been our president."

"HE didn't have the votes," Milo said.

Tears filled my eyes. "I couldn't even hang on to my stock of MREs," I said. The last colony seemed like an impossible dream.

"Don't lose hope," Skinny Liz said. She was walking very close to me now, and she began to gently blot my tears with one of her new dress socks. "It's not all doom and gloom."

"It literally is," I said.

"No. There's still good in this world." She leaned in and whispered in my ear, "*He* has returned and walks among us." Liz seemed to be waiting for me to give her a high five or something, but I wasn't sure how to respond to this.

"Um, are you talking about Jesus?" I asked.

"Nope," Liz said. "I'm talking about the one who is always preparing."

"I guess I'm not familiar."

"You will be. You all will be soon. And when he announces his presence among us all will be well." Liz smiled with creepy ecstatic joy. We'd heard similar things from Smokey Joe and other drifters who'd made their way through our boat camp and just kind of brushed it off. Milo and Cerise and I seemed to be the only agnostics left on the face of the earth.

"Oh please," Cerise said.

"Rejoice in the good news!" Liz said. "Already his arrows of wrath have felled the mighty. He is coming to put his house in order."

"Maybe that seems plausible under the terms of your religion," I said, wanting to be diplomatic. "And no disrespect to your beliefs, but I just don't see that happening, not in a literal way. This," I said, pointing to the smoking ruin outside the smashed up windows, "isn't a one person problem." I finished the Big Red. "He can't do a thing about it, whoever he is."

Liz was getting mad. "Guys, let's just take a breath," Milo said. "We're all friends here. Skinny Liz, I love your faith. I love the way you hold on to what you believe in even in these difficult times. Eric did the same thing for years, didn't you man? You said *the day is at hand and will soon be here* and what have you, and everybody laughed. But now they're not laughing. So maybe Liz's boy will show up. I kind of hope he does."

Liz stopped under a house that was nothing but frame and foundation, and turned her attention to Milo. She filled him in on this savior character she was expecting, all his mighty attributes and how best to honor him and so forth. Cerise and I pantomimed vomiting behind their backs. As we parted ways, she invited us to services in the evening.

"We'll try to be there," Milo promised.

* * *

After another hour walking in circles, we found a faded billboard that read *Future Site of the Don Cheevers Planned Community* but there was no community in evidence. An electric fence ringed the perimeter—the sign said DANGER HIGH VOLTAGE—but there was nobody inside. The whole place seemed deserted.

"They must be below ground," Cerise said. She paced the fence's perimeter, yelling for Hank, but there was no response.

Milo was battling a mix of emotions. He had claimed he was ready to come clean with Hank and beg his forgiveness, but his girlfriend's eagerness to see her husband again was obviously hurtful.

"Touch the fence Eric," she said.

"No way," I said, but she shoved me hard and I fell into it. There was no shock. I did not sizzle against the wire like a strip of bacon.

"We can just cut through it," Cerise said.

It took *forever* to make a hole big enough for us to pass through, using Cerise's pocket knife, and Milo was no help at all. While we worked, he stayed on his knees in the dirt mouthing silent prayers, and he even poured a small libation of Big Red to the new deity. I couldn't believe what I was seeing. I assumed at first that he was joking around, but he bit my head off when I began to sing a sarcastic hymn. Milo's irony quotient was lower, his need to really believe in something far greater. He had undergone an authentic conversion experience back there.

When the hole was finished Cerise began to crawl through it.

"You guys go on ahead," I said. There were blank spaces in my memory thanks to the boy with the bat, but I recalled vividly that Hank Schoenfeld and I had not parted on good terms. He had rigged the apocalypse game for himself and against me, and now he was a person of consequence in the new order, and I'd be expected to bow and scrape before him. I was a loser who couldn't protect my family whereas he had proved himself a doomsday prepper worth the name. No way was I going in there.

"I'm not coming either," Milo said, planting his feet. He hadn't given up on the Gulf, and the electric fence made him skittish. If somebody powered it up, it would function like a mosquito zapper when the waters rolled in, electrocuting everyone at once.

Milo stayed outside the perimeter with his arms crossed. "We need to talk, Cerise. I want to sort all this out. No more hiding, no more lies. I want to know that I matter to you." His voice was breaking. It was very uncomfortable. "I want to know that you're going to tell him about us before I take one more step."

"Come in or he dies," Cerise said, gesturing casually my direction with one of her shotguns.

"She wouldn't," Milo said, but I had an entirely different read on what Cerise was capable of, and I was already pushing him through the fence hole. We found the door to the shelter and climbed down the rickety stairs toward the underground condos. It was too quiet;. I knew it from the moment my foot hit the first step. There were many doors with fancy looking steel numbers, but they opened up into empty space. There was exactly one finished condo, the same one Hank had taken me to—it was the model, evidently—and when Cerise put her fist to the wall in a fit of rage, she busted right through it. My backward pipe shelter had been miles ahead in terms of construction and quality.

Blaine's neighbor Andrea had called it. Don Cheevers was a con artist.

* * *

The walk back to camp was grim. Cerise and I hardly said a word, but Milo chattered on about *the one who is always preparing* and how if we turned to him now, if we truly believed, he would fell the rednecks and save us all.

We heard the horses halfway back to the camp, on an open stretch of cooled lava. There was no cover in sight. Thehorses were getting louder, coming toward us behind a slight hill, and we couldn't see them yet. Milo put his ear to the road like a guy in a Western and listened. Cerise rolled her eyes.

"How many?" I asked. We were in an open stretch of road and there was nowhere to hide.

"Honestly, it sounds like just one really enormous horse," Milo said.

That was wishful thinking. *Two* really enormous horses pulling a cart blew past us. Their terrifying drivers wore helmets with grills made of human teeth. They paid no attention to the three of us, who were hacking and gagging in all the ash the hooves and wheels kicked up. The cart they pulled was packed with human beings, and as the miserable faces of the doomed rolled by, I saw that staring out at me from the back was Lisa.

* * *

"Man, wait. Let's get a posse together first," Milo said. The sight of our fellow residents loaded up like cattle had brought him back to his senses. There had been ample opportunities as of late for a higher power to intervene in human events, but in spite of the newfound popularity of libations and hymns, in spite of the horrors that were now commonplace among us, the higher powers were doing squat. But we'd always known this, Milo and I. Our survival was in our own hands and it always had been.

"Milo, you get who you can. I'm going now."

* * *

The barracks were full of prisoners, packed in tight, and I couldn't see Lisa in that miserable crowd. Well-fed men with long guns were streaming into the Alamo. The mission's hump had collapsed onto the bricks below, but it still stood. The plaza was cracked and uneven from the shifting ground, and small geysers of fire shot up from tiny fissures in the earth. I kept the collar of my shirt across my mouth to keep the groundsmoke out of my lungs.

The Rodneys were standing guard around the perimeter, looking sharp in their paramilitary outfits, but I shuffled through the doors with the crowd and nobody stopped me. The mood was festive, like a sales convention, and people shook hands and introduced themselves, comparing notes and dropping names. One name kept coming up—Hank S. Crockett. That was who everybody was here to see.

Bat Rodney called for silence and said he was proud to introduce the man with the plan, father of the new Texas, Hank Crockett! To my absolute disgust, Hank Schoenfeld strolled in from the side door and the crowd went wild. His hair was longer, and he was sporting a beard that would have made even Milo feel inadequate, along with one of the helmets the riders wore. Human teeth lined his forehead like bangs.

"I have just one question." Hank crossed his arms over his burly chest and studied the crowd. "Why should you trust me?"

"You shouldn't!" I yelled, but a man with a tattoo of the Virgen de Guadalupe punched me in the gut and I fell to the floor, the wind knocked out of me.

The disturbance hadn't registered at the front of the room, and Hank continued, while I struggled to breathe and return myself to an upright position. "You've heard a lot of things. At a time like this, a lot of people come out of the woodwork and say: 'I'm the guy. Follow me.'"

He chuckled. "Let me tell you the difference between those guys and me. I flew in to be here. Understand? I took the last plane into Texas—ask my pilot Mark if you doubt me. Mark, where are you?"

Mark waved from under the flags that jutted out from the wall. "That was a hell of a flight. Let's all give Mark a round of applause." We all hooted and clapped, even me, because the guy with the Guadalupe tattoo had an eye on me.

"While other guys were hunkering down in their coward holes, throwing up their hands and saying *It's the end of the world!* I was thinking." Hank tapped his skull, to illustrate the abstract concept of cogitation for his audience. "Because you can't prepare for doomsday. *Can you prepare for doomsday?*" Hank demanded in his thundering twang.

"No!" the crowd roared.

"Such things are out of the hands of man. Baby, when it's over, it's over. But I'm here to tell you, this is just the beginning." Hank's speech had more applause lines than the state of the union. I was doing the minimum to keep from getting my ass kicked, but already my palms were numb.

"We aren't beaten. We're down but we're not out. And don't tell me what the experts say about the state of this planet. Don't tell me what you can't do. Don't tell me it's too hard. Because I say bull!" Now we were stomping our feet, too.

"We are launching a new Texas here today and each and every one of you is a part of it. It's going to be bigger. It's going to be better. We will return to the values of our forebears and we will survive. We will endure. We will not be beholden to weaklings and pessimists. We will rise again from these ashes, brothers!"

My throat was getting raw from screaming my full-throated assent to Hank's drivel, and I was relieved to see he was winding up.

"I'll address you again later. Now let's break into small groups—see your team leader if you're unsure of your small group assignment. Be sure to stop by the expo booths because we have got some very exciting products on offer. And don't forget to get yourself a plate of barbecue!"

We screamed "Crockett, Crockett, Crockett!" and clapped and stomped our feet like the bunch of jerks we were, and then we poured out into the plaza.

* * *

I hadn't eaten meat besides poultry since *before*, and the smell of woodsmoke and beef was intoxicating. I fell in line behind some men in helmets and waited my turn.

"What's your team?" the cook said, looking askance at my crossbow.

"The two-steppers," I said, guessing. It was a good guess. He handed me a plate and I began to devour it. It tasted so good it brought tears to my eyes. When I had cleaned my plate I made my way toward the barracks to find Lisa. A shapely human thigh was turning on a spit, and the cooks were cutting slices from it. In my opinion, it belonged to a pear-shaped woman under 5'5. "That's fresh," a man said, smacking his lips.

When I saw the birthmark near the ankle, I vomited.

"You can't do that here," one of the Rodneys said, poking me in the back with the butt of his gun. "If you're diseased you got to clear out."

"Lisa!" I screamed.

"I *said* clear out." The Rodney kicked me and I fell over, still screaming.

"Eric Estrada," Hank said, crossing the plaza to confront me. "How in the hell are you still alive?"

* * *

Hank was extremely amused to see me again and delighted to find that I was faring very badly in the new order. He was more than content with how things had panned out. The Don Cheevers had been a disappointment, as had Cerise's betrayal, but he was determined to stay positive. "I'm not going to lie down in the ash and die. I'm a leader, and a leader leads."

"But where are you leading them, Hank?" I didn't care that I was crying. It was just a matter of time, probably no more than half an hour, before Hank finished gloating and smashed my head against the nearest wall.

To my surprise, Hank choked up too. "I want the same things you want. I want my family back. My life back." He cried without shame, like a football coach at a press conference, just sobbing away. He sniffed loudly and pulled himself together. "But I won't get my family back. Cormac is dead, and my wife is in love with a millennial." His pain was palpable. A man who once proudly rode a fixed geared bicycle in a bowler hat had usurped his wife's affections. No wonder Hank now commanded a loose militia of cannibals under an assumed name: he had no self-respect left at all.

"I'm not sure it's *love*, exactly," I said recalling how she'd threatened Milo with her shotguns and used him to pay a bar tab, but Hank's face clouded over with rage. Nobody wants to hear his wife's affair is strictly a physical matter. "Well," I said, feeling awkward. "These are crazy times. Please make it quick," I said.

"Your death? Oh, hell no. I'm thinking something more in the prolonged category."

* * *

My new blue uniform was too big and the kitchen was dirty and chaotic. Thigh bones protruded from under the lid of a Dutch oven. A rancid smell of garbage and spoiled meat hung over everything. I was on staff at the Alamo now, stewing up the less palatable trimmings that weren't worthy of the barbecue pits. It wasn't easy, but our shift manager Gary liked my positive attitude and the way I put my back into it when I dragged the dirty mop over the filthy bricks. "You won't stay on the sludge line for long, Estrada. You are destined for better things."

"Thank you, sir. I certainly hope so," I'd said. I'd already earned a reputation as a kiss-ass, thanks to that remark, and I'd only been on crew for two and a half hours. I hated myself for that, for my inability to quit trying. Whatever miserable workplace I found myself in, even this one, I threw myself into it with everything I had. I just couldn't break the habit of trying to scramble to the top, and I looked forward to the day Hank would break it for me, by scrambling my brains on the pavement. My colleague Tanya was wiping at the dishes with a dirty sponge, singing a hymn.

"So does anyone ever escape from the barracks?" I said, poking a spoon into a bubbling pot of don't ask, don't tell stew. I'd begun to hope the leg hadn't been Lisa's after all. Wasn't it a little longer than hers? Wasn't her birthmark slightly higher up from the ankle? I knew that only the truly deranged were capable of this kind of chipper optimism, but I couldn't beat back these hopeful thoughts, even as I labored in a kitchen full of gore. I supposed that when I'd bitten into those tender slices of human brisket I had gone completely insane.

"Nope," Tanya said. "Nobody gets out of the barracks. Only the ghosts."

"The what?"

"The ghosts," Tanya said, smacking chewing gum that she made herself from tendon and cartilage.

"You see them too?" I said. "I thought I was the only one."

* * *

On our break, Tanya led me to the backside of the Alamo. "There's a real good one here. It's strong stuff, so go easy," Tanya said. "The last guy completely flipped. You've got to build up a tolerance."

"I can handle it," I said. I bent over the fissure and filled my lungs with groundsmoke. The air began to shimmer. I breathed in again. I wanted to see Lisa one more time. My lungs were aching but I exhaled and bent over the fissure. I sucked up as much groundsmoke as I could stand, more than I'd ever breathed in before. The empty space around me began to fill.

"Easy," Tanya cautioned, but I ignored her. I took one last huff and stood up, filling dizzy and sick. Every square inch of the plaza was packed with the dead. Mexican regimentals, Franciscan priests, Payaya families, a smattering of tourists who'd died of heatstroke on vacation, still holding bags of commemorative Alamo merchandise.

Blaine Raddax was standing with his pants unzipped, splashing the shrine of Texas liberty with his ghostly urine. "Show some respect," I chided his ghost, but he just grinned at me. "What happened to you, man?" I said.

"I got killed!" Blaine said. He was as surprised as I. "Real bad earthquake right after you guys left. So yeah, I'm dead. But I'm not going to let that change me."

"I'm looking for Lisa," I said. I was having trouble standing upright.

"You need to take it easy on the groundsmoke, buddy. This whole place is going under like *real soon* and you better sober up, because I don't think you're prepared."

"I'm never prepared," I said bitterly.

"One of the downsides of the incorporeal lifestyle is that I am now unable to slap some sense into you. Haven't you heard the good news about the one who is always prepared?"

"Yes," I said. "I can't believe you buy into that."

"I *wrote* that. I wrote that for you, Estrada. You're the guy. It's my first posthumous hit." Blaine sang a few verses, as I stood staring at him, too smoked up to move. It was no wonder that the cult's adherents were all people who enjoyed groundsmoke and that the hymns had a relentless rhythm and extremely loud vocals. They were getting their information from the ghost of a last gasp metal frontman.

"I've got to find Lisa," I said and I staggered toward the barracks. I passed General Santa Anna, who was loitering in his epaulettes, on the way. We exchanged bows.

When I reached the barracks, Parker Saenz was there, fiddling with the lock. "You'll need your bow," she said, passing it to me. "First Hank, then as many as you can."

I reached out to hug her and found I was trying to throw my arms around a flock of squawking black grackles.

* * *

Hank was in a meeting with his team leaders, dividing up what remained of Texas' land between his underlings. I shot him in the throat as he assigned West Texas to a man named Abe who was wearing a necklace of finger bones.

"The cattle are loose!" someone screamed and the men grabbed their guns and ran to the barracks, which Parker had opened. Prisoners were streaming out. Amid the chaos, I shot as many of Hank's guys in the back as I could.

* * *

"Lisa, I thought I lost you," I said. She was embracing our daughters and Elias. We were aboard *The Jolly Barista*, which Milo had driven down with the last of his truck's gas. Milo had rallied nearly all of Trip Edmond's farm to the cause and three other boats were assembled outside the Alamo, packed with whoever was rash enough to follow a malnourished baker into a naval battle on dry land. We heard snickering from inside the mission, where what remained of Hank's team was holed up. We looked like fools, but I tried not to be critical.

"It's a classic stand-off," Elias said. "But they've got the numbers and the guns. We're going to die in these boats."

"There's always hope," I said. I was still pretty blitzed on groundsmoke and there was a roaring in my ears like the wind of the gulf".

* * *

"Who called it? *Who* called it?" Milo said, strutting across the deck in his captain's hat. "I hate to say I told you so, but I did." There was nothing but ocean in all directions and we had long conceded his point. A more mature person would have dropped it by now.

"You called it, Milo," I said, for the hundredth time. We'd been at sea three days and he was still celebrating. Even Cerise found his high spirits insufferable and she had threatened several times to throw herself overboard.. Then the two of them would argue, and Milo would end up apologizing, and then they'd start kissing passionately in a corner of the boat, turning everyone's stomachs even more than the choppy seas.

"I wish you'd left me to die," Elias said, shaking his head as Cerise swept Milo into a backbend kiss.

* * *

"It's kind of embarrassing, Lees, but you know this new god everyone's so into lately? I'm kind of worried that it's *me*," I whispered. We were standing on deck together, watching the garbage islands float past.

Lisa gave me a look so full of contempt that my heart melted. It was just like the old days. "You can't just be normal, Eric. You always have to have some crazy delusion."

"I know I'm just an ordinary guy. I know that. But think about it—the mighty archer? The one who is always prepared? The one who walks among us, as in *door to door?*"

"Honestly, I'm embarrassed for you," she said.

"It sounds bad. But all these mighty deeds he supposedly did? Like half of them are mine. I don't know if I should say something or let it go or what." Blaine had been writing my life story into his posthumous hits, and whenever somebody poured a libation to the mighty archer or fasted so as to win his favor I felt guilty.

"That one right there could be land," Lisa said, pointing to a dark streak on the horizon. Birds had been flying over us for two days, and the way they didn't nose dive onto the deck and die gave us hope. Lisa had agreed to name the baby Milo, which worked well for either a boy or a girl, but that was before we had any reason to expect we'd live to see the child born. I wanted to pin her down on the name now that our outlook had improved from *certain death* to *small but significant chance of survival.*

"I've got it. Milo Santa Anna," I said.

"That's bizarre," Lisa said. But we weren't bound by the old ways anymore. We could do what we wanted. We ate fish that we hoped was not slowly poisoning us and we planned to raise our children in peace and freedom, never knowing first-hand the taste of human flesh. (Which, for the record: *excellent.*) "Why would you want to name our baby after that jackass?"

I wasn't sure which jackass she meant, or how much Lisa was ready to hear. But I confessed that on that day, at what we were calling the second battle of the Alamo, just before the gulf poured in and drowned the defenders, General Santa Anna had tipped his hat to me. Then he had raised his arm and at his command, the water seeped up from the ground beneath our boats, flooding the plaza. The waves that crashed over the Alamo were full of soldiers on horseback, carrying the flag of Mexico. "I saw it all, just like I see you now. It was that clear."

"You were pretty high, though," Lisa said.

"Yes I was," I said. Lisa kissed me as we sailed past a garbage island made of rubber ducks.

The End

Eileen Curtright lives in San Antonio, Texas, with her husband and three daughters. Her novel *The Burned Bridges of Ward, Nebraska,* is forthcoming in November 2015.

Paleo

Paleo

Pete waited four weeks before going across the street to talk to the new neighbor. It made no sense that this guy would want his property to look like shit, and Pete was content to believe that sooner or later the problem would fix itself. It didn't, and Jenny kept looking out the window, and then glaring at Pete like it was *his* fault, like Pete was the only thing in the universe standing in the way of her happiness.

Pete had enough to worry about, and he had a hard time seeing how this was on him. Some guy decided to buy the McMansion across the street and let his yard turn into a jungle. Sure, it looked terrible, but who, when you really thought about it, gave a crap? Jenny for one, but she wasn't about to actually take matters into her own hands. Pete figured eventually one of the other neighbors would speak to the guy, but as far as he could tell, no one did.

The breaking point came for Pete when they went over to the Hudsons' for dinner on Friday night. Jenny had been best friends with Lola Hudson back in high school, when she was Lola Macklin. She'd been sort of a mousy thing then, like Jenny had been, but Lola had discovered sluttiness at A&M and caught the eye of Rick Hudson, with whom they'd gone to school their whole lives. He'd never noticed the old Lola, with her glasses and messy hair hidden under sweatshirt hoods, but he liked the new one with contact lenses and exposed cleavage and circus-act high heels.

They got hitched shortly after graduation and moved back to San Antonio. Jenny, who was married to Pete by then, resumed the old friendship. That meant Pete had to pretend that Rick had not spent all of high school, and much of middle school, acting like a total asshole. It wasn't that Rick had bullied Pete – good fucking luck with that. Once in a while, someone would get it into his head that Pete, who had been on the quiet side, was easy prey. He'd been wiry and slender back then, but strong as hell, and anyone who got in his face regretted it. Rick hadn't been much of a brawler, but he'd had an attitude like he'd known all along that he was going places and Pete wasn't. *Contempt* was the word. Rick had always treated Pete with contempt. Now the two of them were supposed to be pals.

Pete had never really planned much for the future, and he'd more or less stumbled into the home inspection business. Rick, meanwhile, had majored in geology and right after graduation he went to work for one of the big oil companies. They now had a huge house in Alamo Heights, which Pete found distasteful to visit, drive past, discuss, or picture in his mind. He hated how Rick loved playing the host, taking out some new prize bottle of scotch or wine that he could show off and casually mention which politician had sent it to him as a gift or how much it had cost at auction. He hated how he would show off some modification they'd done to the house or the pool or the guest house. Then Rick would say, "So, what's happening at your homestead?" and he would smile because he knew that jackshit was happening at Pete's homestead. Pete's homestead wasn't changing any time soon. They weren't going to be adding a hot tub or a wine cellar or a fucking solarium.

Pete would say that things were the same as they always were, but now even this had become a lie. Things were not nearly that good, but he wasn't about to admit that to Rick. He hadn't even come clean to Jenny.

After dinner, Chilean sea bass – "Thirty-two dollars a pound," Rick told them, "and there's plenty of it!" – prepared and served by an equally Chilean housekeeper, the four of them sat in the living room in the glow of Rick's 70 gallon saltwater aquarium. Rick had a guy come in once a week to maintain it, he liked to say just about every time they came over. Who, he wanted to know, could be bothered to do it themselves? But it looked great, right? Right?

Jenny and Lola had huddled off into their own conversation, as inevitably happened. These girl-chats came in two varieties: the loud and explosive giggles, which annoyed Pete, or the serious, staccato whispers, which terrified him. Even worse, with the wives having self-exiled, Pete was left alone with Rick, who swirled his *postprandial* scotch around his glass and sniffed at it and nodded his approval.

Rick, on top of everything else, was still fit and had all his hair. Pete, by contrast, had gained fifty pounds since high school and the hair was beginning to recede. Maybe it had already receded. He thought he had a shrinking hairline, but the week before he'd heard one of his daughter's friends describe him as *bald*. Rick was getting stronger and richer and better looking. Pete was getting fatter and poorer and more pathetic. Most of the time he could convince himself that this was just life. This was what happened. You couldn't be like someone on a TV show because those people were made up. Then he would come over to Rick's house and he would be reminded that it wasn't just fantasy. Some people really did live that way – people he knew, people with whom he'd gone to high school, people who had made different choices.

"I heard you have a problem with your new neighbor?" Rick was saying as he sniffed at his scotch.

"How'd you hear that?" Pete asked. He took an experimental sip of the drink and tried not to wince. Scotch, in his opinion, tasted like complete shit. The good stuff tasted like a different kind of shit than the bad stuff, but none of it tasted like anything Pete ever wanted to put inside of his mouth. And it wasn't like Pete was some kind of moron who couldn't tell the difference between quality liquor and the cheap stuff. He knew a kick ass bourbon when he tasted one, and he knew Rick had a few bottles of a pricey small batch sitting around. Pete had suggested they switch over to bourbon a few visits ago, but Rick had just said, "Nah," and waved his hand and grinned with content triumph, as if to say you never had so much power that you could feel comfortable giving up even a little.

"This is killer, right?" Rick said, holding up his glass. "A little gift from my inside guy over at the Railroad Commissioner's Office."

"Tastes like smoke," Pete said, having long since learned the right bullshit terms. "And peat." Why the fuck anyone would want to drink something that tasted like smoke and peat was beyond him.

"So what's the deal with the guy across the street?" Rick asked.

Pete sighed. There was no avoiding the conversation. "He won't cut his lawn. It's overgrown like crazy."

"Damn, that's no good. What do your neighbors say?"

Pete shrugged. He didn't know the neighbors anymore. The house on Laurel Lane had belonged to his parents, who moved to Arizona fifteen years ago and gave it to Pete and Jenny outright. Back when they'd first taken ownership, the neighborhood had been an actual community. Everyone had known everyone else. Pete and Jenny had gone to high school with half the people on the block. Now, all his friends had sold and moved, and Pete was the last man standing. More than that, his was one of the last houses standing. Most of the modest ranch houses had been torn down, replaced by 6,000 square foot behemoths that strained against the confines of their lots. His new neighbors – lawyers and doctors and real estate developers – squinted at Pete when he pulled into his driveway in his seven-year-old Honda like he didn't belong there, like he was bringing down the neighborhood. Pete *was* the neighborhood. That's what they didn't get.

"I don't really talk to the neighbors," Pete said. He heard himself wincing, like he knew he was going to get blasted for this. When had this happened to him? When had he become the guy who hunched his shoulders and waited for the blows to land? He took another sip of the disgusting and expensive scotch to try to ward off the feeling of absolute and utter defeat.

This, he decided, was life. In high school he'd had a pretty good circle of friends. People respected how he could beat the shit out of pretty much anyone, but he never started a fight. He didn't talk a lot, like Clint Eastwood, and he was content with himself. Some kids found that magnetic. Now he was just a guy pushing forty whose life had become a daily struggle, and no one seemed particularly drawn to *that*.

Rick snapped him out of this reflection by slamming his hand on the coffee table. "Dude," he pronounced with great sadness and concern. "You've got to work the neighbors. On my block, I'm king shit. No one plants a flower bed without getting my say so."

"I don't really want to tell anyone what they can or can't—"

"I'm not telling them," Rick explained, helpfully cutting Pete off. His voice had gone slower and higher pitched, like he was telling a child about how the moon was really a rock in space or some shit. "At least, they don't *know* I am. I mean, they think they're coming to me for advice, and then they think they're doing what they want to do. That's the key to good management. I guess, working alone, you don't really need skills like that."

"I guess not," Pete agreed because it seemed like a better move than breaking his glass against Rick's face.

"You ever think about expanding? Turning that small business into a medium-sized business? I can talk you through it. Give you some pointers. No charge. Just, you know, when you make it, maybe it can be *your* expensive hooch we're drinking for a change."

Rick did his *I'm joking, but I'm really not, because I'm a complete dick* laugh. Pete smiled because that's what good manners required, but he felt like a dog lowering its head in submission.

"What do you say?" Rick gave Pete a shove on one shoulder, as if to push him into prosperity. "You ready to make the leap?"

"I'm doing just fine the way things are," Pete said, which was absolutely not true. He was not doing fine. Business had all but evaporated since the lawsuit, which was not going away, and was likely going to crush him if things didn't change soon. Jenny didn't know about any of this because it had all exploded in the last month, but she was going to find out sooner or later. The way she and Lola stopped whispering and turned to look at him made him wonder if she already suspected that something was wrong. That look on her face wasn't suspicion, though. They'd been married too long for him to misunderstand the twist of her eyebrows and the lines around her mouth.

It was disappointment.

"First thing," Rick said, finishing his scotch and slamming it down like a cowboy in a saloon, "you have to talk to your neighbor. Let him know what's what. Act like you're a fucking man, then you'll feel like one. And then you'll *be* one."

Jenny looked up, still locked in her housewife huddle. Her eyebrows were knit, her mouth pursed. It was impossible to tell if she was talking to Lola or the men. "That would be nice," she said, her voice very quiet.

* * *

The house was beautiful, a Spanish style fortress whose former inhabitants had built and lived in it for a year before selling. Pete had not spoken to them once. The new guy had hired landscapers to put in new shrubs along the stone walkway, and the BMW sports car in the circular driveway always glistened as if just washed, so Pete could not make any sense of the lawn. It hadn't been mowed once during his neighbor's four weeks in the house. In spite of the drought, and the water restrictions, the neighbor had been running his sprinklers three times a week. It was like he *wanted* the grass to grow.

The next morning around eleven o'clock Pete told Jenny he was walking over.

"Already?" she asked, looking up from her laptop, where he suspected she was shopping for things she would later complain about not being able to afford. Jenny liked to buy certain items online, mostly makeup, cookware, athletic clothes, vitamins, storage containers, handbags, scarves, and decorative objects made out of pink glass that would live out their days in boxes stacked in the garage. "You don't want to wait a few more weeks?"

In recent years, Jenny had evidently come to find nagging so enjoyable that she couldn't see any reason to stop, even after it had served its purpose. Pete didn't want to get into a fight, so he just shook his head.

Then Jenny looked up and smiled at him, and it was the smile that made him think that the old Jenny was still in there, that their relationship was not lost forever. That smile was kind and warm and genuine. It said she saw things in him that no one else could be bothered to see. "It won't be so bad," she said.

Like Pete, she was 38, but she looked a whole lot better than he did. She kept herself trim, she'd dyed her hair blonde, and wore it in a casual ponytail. Like her friends whose husbands made more money than Pete, Jenny favored designer athletic clothes whether or not any actual athletic activity was in the forecast. Now she stood, hips cocked, eyes wide, smile mischievous. She looked good.

"I'm sure it won't," he said.

"Be firm," she told him. "Don't let him push you around."

"I know how to talk to people," he said.

"Of course you do. Maybe you should take Addison. He'll probably be nicer if she's there."

Addison was their 12-year-old daughter, currently in the throes of early-onset moody adolescence. The last thing he wanted was to bring a disaffected tween who would scowl and roll her eyes and do a kabuki dance of boredom and embarrassment while Pete tried to politely explain to his neighbor that the front lawn of Downton fucking Abbey should not look like the Mekong Delta.

Her personal-effrontery detector always cranked to maximum, Addison now appeared at their bedroom doorway. She was tall and thin and pale-skinned and on her way to being a genuine beauty, though currently she suffered from a bit of giraffey awkwardness. Jenny wished she would grow out of it, but Pete found it endearing. He was in no rush to let go of the last traces of her childhood.

"I'm not going," Addison announced with finality. Then she added, "Where?"

"Walk across the street with your father," Jenny said. "You can be his human shield while he talks to the neighbor."

Addison must have sensed the possibility for drama because she allowed herself a slight smile. "Okay."

* * *

They stood before the massive oak double doors, ornately carved like the entrance to a medieval keep, and Pete jammed his finger into the glowing amber bubble of the doorbell. In the distance they heard the multi-note chime, not the standard ding, but a fanfare to alert the footman that a gentleman had come to call. There was a long pause, then the scrape of feet, followed by the science-fictional beeping of the alarm system being told to stand down and, finally, the heavy thud of impenetrable locks unbolting. The door swung inward and Pete got his first glimpse of his new neighbor.

Much to Pete's dismay, he looked like an action movie hero. The guy was probably six-two, in his early thirties, with a full head of hair, and a handsome, cover-of-*Men's-Health* face. He wore jeans and a black t-shirt, and there was no mistaking that this guy was in fantastic shape. Veins like tree roots lined his arms, and under his sleeves his biceps looked like balloons ready to burst.

"Yeah," he said. "What?"

Pete glanced over at Addison, who had her ear buds in place and was fiddling with her iPhone. That, at least, was good. He didn't want his daughter to see this meathead be an asshole to her father.

"Hey, there," he said. "I just wanted to talk to you about your grass."

The guy shook his head. "I'm not hiring anyone right now. Leave me a card or something."

It took Pete a few seconds to recover. The guy thought he wanted to mow the lawn? Had something happened since Pete last looked in the mirror that would make this guy think he was a Mexican? Not that there was anything wrong with looking Mexican – or being Mexican for that matter. Pete, who considered himself enlightened, believed Mexican was an okay thing to be if that was how the dice rolled for you, but he was a white guy who looked like nothing but a white guy, and he lived in a town where no white guy over the age of 17 had mowed a lawn for money since before Prohibition.

Treat the guy like a client, Pete told himself. Be a businessman, focus on the goal. The goal was that everyone should think they were being treated fairly. He took a deep breath to steady himself. "I'm Pete. I live across the street."

"And?" the man inquired.

Pete forced a laugh. He was being a friendly guy, controlling the tone of the conversation. "So, now one of us knows who the other is."

The man stared at him for a long time, his expression utterly neutral. "William Casey," he said. He did not offer Pete a hand.

"Okay, Will," Pete tried. "Bill? Billy?"

"William," said William.

"Okay, William," continued Pete, who was still reeling from having his efforts to be friendly thrown back at him. Riding out the conversational turbulence was not going to get him anything, so he figured he might as well get to the point. "The thing is, your lawn is kind of overgrown."

"It's *my* lawn," William said. "It can be whatever length I like."

"Yeah, well, it's ugly, and I have to look at it."

William looked Pete up and down, like he was noting the weight, the hair loss, the clothes, the extra decade, the thousands of subtle signs that, of the two of them, he made a lot less money – all of the things Pete hated most about himself. He opened his mouth, and then said nothing, only pressed his lips together as if pleased with himself for walking away from the low hanging fruit.

Pete felt himself actually growing dizzy under the weight of the implied insult, all the more terrible for having been left unspoken. He glanced over at Addison, and she was staring at William and he could see that she had gotten it. She understood.

There was no way he was going to let this douchebag humiliate him in front of his daughter. It was time to push back – not grow a pair. He was not about to use Rick's bullshit lingo, even to himself. Besides, he didn't need to grow anything. He'd always had a pair.

"We live in a nice neighborhood," Pete said. "This isn't a frat house, and you can't treat your place like a batch pad because you're not the only one affected by letting the property deteriorate. You need to mow your lawn, William, and you need to do it this weekend."

Pete had scored. He had been direct and forceful, and he had schooled this punk. He looked directly into the asshole's eyes and dared him to back down.

William did not look away. "I am letting it grow for religious reasons."

This, admittedly, was something Pete had not seen coming. Laziness or territorial pissing, like the sort of thing Rick would do, made sense to him. But not this. "Are you Jewish? Is this like growing a beard or something?"

William did not say anything.

"Because, that's fine if you are," Pete continued, now trying to feel his way through unknown territory. "I completely believe in being tolerant of other religions."

"That's great that you are willing to tolerate other people, Pete. That is super swell." Somehow the fact that he hadn't altered his tone made him sound even more contemptuous.

Pete turned to Addison, who continued to watch these developments with great interest. He needed to take control of the conversation again.

"What religion, exactly, is this that makes you turn your house into an eyesore for the entire neighborhood?"

"A very old one," William said. "And frankly it's none of your business."

"It is my business," Pete said, "because I have to look out the window every day and see—"

William now took a step forward. Involuntarily, Pete took a step back, and he could see Addison watching him, a smirk on her face.

"Honestly," William said, "I don't give a crap about what you have to look at and what you don't. I am purifying my home according to my religious beliefs, and if you don't like that, you can feel free to fuck off. Any questions?"

Pete stood in stunned silence. William turned back into his house and closed the door, calmly, not slamming it, as though this encounter hadn't even made him truly angry. Pete heard the turning of the locks and the leisurely shuffle of withdrawing footsteps.

Though it was the last thing he wanted to do, he risked a look at Addison, whose face had blossomed into full smirk.

"He's totally cute," she said.

* * *

Back at their house, Addison went inside, and Pete mumbled something about having to check on the sprinklers. The thing was, he couldn't just let this go. Douchebag William, as he had already begun to think of his neighbor, had been rude and dismissive, and that annoyed him, but it was par for the course these days. Pete was used to his rich neighbors wrinkling their noses as they walked their dogs past his house. He took a strange sort of pride in it, though he wasn't sure he could have explained why. No, this was something different. The neighbor had seemed off. Something wasn't right over there.

Without even knowing what he was doing, or exactly why, he crossed back over to the house and found himself standing on the front porch, finger poised over the doorbell like a viper ready to strike. Except he did not want to ring. Douchebag William would come back and get annoyed and act superior. Or maybe he wouldn't even answer the door at all. There was no point in creating a conflict that Douche Will could win simply by not showing up. What Pete wanted was to have something on the guy.

The neighbor had dismissed him, compared him to a Mexican, and closed the door in his face. Pete had heard him walk off, but he had not heard the security system re-arm. Why bother? William was awake, and it was daytime and he was a manly man. He didn't need to cower inside his own house. There was no reason he needed to electronically defend the place.

Which meant there was no reason Pete couldn't have a look in the backyard. Pete inspected homes. There was nothing more natural or ordinary for him than walking onto a stranger's property. If he were caught, he could just say he saw something odd in the foundation and wanted to check it out – to be neighborly.

He walked around the side of the house, along the slate path lined by lush foliage and loquat trees weighted down by fruit a week or so shy of ripening. He reached the wooden gate and gave the handle a test pull. It was latched. On the other side of the gate, defending the security of William's backyard, was a metal hook.

This was no surprise. Pete had seen these things a thousand times. He'd circumvented them almost as often. People generally forgot to unlatch their gates, and if Pete needed to get into the yard, he could either go back through the house or he could do what he was doing now – find a narrow twig, slide it between the planks of wood, and lift the latch. No big deal.

The yard was typical of the oversized houses in the neighborhood. The buildings themselves took up the overwhelming bulk of the lot, and all that was left was a sliver of land. William hadn't done much with it, and the grass, like in the front, had been allowed to grow high. There was a wooden deck with a propane grill and a few chairs. The only thing unusual was the structure at the far end. It was made of planks of unfinished wood, and it stood a good ten feet high and maybe six wide. From Pete's perspective, it was just a rough wooden wall, supported by angled poles that were driven deep into the ground. A plank projected from the top away from Pete, and he couldn't see if it was suspending anything, but from the way the whole structure leaned forward, it seemed to be weighted down.

Pete had a thought, and he made an observation, and these things happened at the same time. The thought was that the structure looked like the back of a makeshift gallows. The observation was the sound of a slow and steady drip. Something was suspended from the structure, something that dripped, and suddenly Pete felt like he should not be there.

He wanted to run. He wanted to get the fuck out of there and never come back, but he willed himself to stay still. He was not some little kid who had to worry about whether or not his neighbor was the boogeyman. He was an adult, and while he had no idea what his asshole neighbor was up to, he felt pretty sure the guy was not conducting executions in his backyard.

He moved a little bit forward, glancing up to see if there were any visible lights on inside the house. It was morning and bright, and there were lots of windows, which meant a light would not necessarily be on, even if Douchebag William were in the room. The implication there, of course, was that the guy could be standing at any one of those windows, watching Pete right now, and he wouldn't know.

Well, fuck him, Pete decided. Let him call the cops if he wants. Rather than sneaking around like he was ashamed of himself, Pete strode forward, carrying himself in a way that suggested he had every right to be there. He peered around the corner of the scaffolding to see what was dangling, what was dripping.

At first he thought it was a dog. It was a long, spindly, gray thing with shaggy looking fur, suspended from the top by one leg. It was skinny, and Pete could see its ribcage jutting through the bloody muscle and tattered fur of its chest.

He eyes followed it down, and came to the neck, which had been cut, roughly, like with an axe. It was jagged and uneven. Bits of sharp bone stuck out, and ribbons of meat hung loose like lolling tongues. And then, a few feet under that, was a metal bucket, slowly filling with the slow dripping of blood. Each drop landing and sending out low vibrations, the way plastic buckets never did.

Off to the side sat the head, propped weirdly on what looked like a department store manikin, the kind with no arms. The plastic head had been removed and the animal's placed there in its stead. It wasn't a dog. It was a goat. Its roughly severed head held in place by some kind of metal spike coming out of the manikin, the glinting base just visible under the fur and gore. Beneath that, along the manikin's heavily muscled shoulders and chest, blood streaked, bright against the sepia plastic.

Then there was what was missing. The flies. Not a single insect buzzed around the goat. There was no buzzing of wings in the air. Just the dripping and, now, Pete's ragged breathing.

Pete felt a jarring cocktail of emotions course through him – shock, disgust, even elation over the discovery that his asshole neighbor was some kind of super freak. More powerful than the rest, however, was fear. Fear like this was some place he should not be – that little boy out of his depth-feeling rising to the top again. He also felt sure – he *knew* – that he was looking at something not meant for him, something that he was not supposed to know about, something that would get him into a kind of unfathomable trouble he dared not even consider.

He was working this out, frozen by all the ideas and the confusion of feelings. He also knew that he wasn't alone. He didn't feel like he was being watched. Not exactly. He didn't think that Douchebag William was up in the house, peering down, thinking, *Oi, that wanker's taking a gander at me dirty work*. Why, in this vision, William had a cockney accent, Pete could not have said. But he did, and it didn't matter, because Pete felt sure William was not watching him. He felt like there were a bunch of people watching him, dozens of them, hidden in the bushes, behind the fence, under the foundation. He felt like he'd wandered into a bar in a strange neighborhood, full of muscled and angry and ethnic types, poor and resentful – men who simply did not give a fuck what happened to them.

Running would be a mistake. They would overtake him. They would come crawling out of their hiding places in the bushes and from behind the fence and under the foundation, and they would grab him with their dozens of hands and they would – he didn't know what. Then he did. He had a clear vision of himself strung up on that makeshift gallows, his own headless neck dripping into the metal bucket, his own head propped on the bloody manikin.

Pete turned away. He walked slowly, deliberately, plotting each step with geometrical precision. He crossed the yard, moving like he'd shit in his pants – which he had not, somehow. He opened the gate, and nothing grabbed him. He closed the gate again, and he was still safe. Continuing to move slowly, as though not wanting to alarm a growling dog, he passed Douchebag William's untamed lawn, crossed the street, and stepped onto his own property.

He expected to feel safe now, like the spell was broken, like he was touching base and nothing could hurt him. But he did not feel safe. He felt frightened out of his fucking mind.

* * *

After Addison's bedtime, Pete sat in the living room with a can of beer in his hand. He'd managed to shake a lot of the fear from what he'd seen in the backyard. It was twisted and disgusting. It was fucked up and probably against city ordinances, but it wasn't really all that terrifying, was it? He'd felt sure it hadn't been that bad when he opened his first Shiner, and now, three beers later, he was pretty close to positive. The whole mess had something to do with whatever insane religion wouldn't let him cut his lawn, which meant the dead goat was no more frightening than a bunch of communion wafers or Muslim man-dresses or whatever the hell else other people used for their strange churches. Pete had briefly considered Googling the overgrown lawn & dead goat religion, but then he decided he would rather not know. Maybe it was Pentecostal or something. He'd known a few of those types, and they were always weird.

Next to him, on the L-shaped sofa, Jenny sipped at a glass of piss-yellow chardonnay she had tapped from the box in the refrigerator. She wore a tennis skirt and a clinging athletic wear top, and she was curled up into herself, legs underneath her in a way Pete could not possibly imagine was comfortable. Maybe it was something that came from always dressing like she was about to go to yoga class.

"So, basically," Jenny said, "the guy blew you off."

Jenny had gone out that morning and been with her friends most of the day. After dinner, once they both had drinks in hand, he'd told her about his encounter with William. He left out the business in the backyard. He tried to tell himself that he had concealed that little detail because he'd been there illegally, and she would have given him shit about it. Maybe there was a time when she would have been impressed, possibly even turned on, by his recklessness, but those days were rooted in the Bush years. But avoiding a fight wasn't why he left it out. It wasn't even because he'd been, at the time, and however irrationally, scared. Any sane person would be disturbed by what Pete had seen. The real reason, he knew, was because he felt like it was a secret, and in the past few weeks, keeping secrets had become second nature.

"He told me he wouldn't cut his lawn because of his religion," Pete said.

"He was jerking you around," Jenny opined. "He was taking advantage of you because you let him."

"If Addison hadn't been there, things could have gone differently, but I couldn't let things get out of control in front of her."

"I suppose," Jenny agreed, studying the contents of her glass like she was reading tea leaves. "You could have sent her home."

He turned to her. "It was your idea that she should come with me."

Jenny smirked. "So it was my fault?"

"I'm just saying."

Jenny pinched her lips together then drank down half her glass. "Meanwhile, we still have to look at that lawn."

Pete took a breath and then stood, threw his beer can in the trash, where it clinked hollowly against its fallen comrades. He went to the refrigerator to grab another. Jenny was giving him shit for no good reason, a pastime she indulged in fairly frequently these days. Pete knew another sort of man might have hit his wife under these circumstances. Certainly his father would have hit his mother, but Pete didn't go into that sort of thing, and he had never hit Jenny. Not once. Not even when any rational man would have hit his wife. He didn't regret it now. Not exactly. Even so, he couldn't help but wonder if they wouldn't both be a lot happier if Jenny had a sense of which lines she ought not to cross.

He sighed, disappointed because he knew he was blaming the wrong person. If he was going to be honest with himself, he had to admit things going tits up with the neighbor hadn't been Jenny's fault. It was her fault she was being a bitch about it now, of course, but that was its own problem. Pete could see why Jenny thought bringing Addison was a good idea, even if it hadn't played out so well. The question now was, how was he going to settle things with Douchebag William? His wife and his daughter thought he couldn't get things done. His last shreds of authority were eroding away, and when Jenny found out about the lawsuit, they were going to be gone forever. He had to act. He had to turn the tide or he was going to lose his family and his business.

Pete yanked the tab off his beer and looked over at Jenny, who had turned on the TV and was flipping through reality TV shows about rich women shouting at one another.

"Don't worry," he said. "I'll deal with this."

Jenny changed the channel and took a sip of her wine like she hadn't heard him or like she hadn't wanted to.

* * *

Home inspectors liked to say that people in their professions came in two camps: those who had been sued, and those who hadn't been sued yet. Homes always had problems, and sometimes buyers didn't understand the reports they signed even though there was a basic concept that said if you signed it, you are pretty much telling the world that you understand it. Still, there's a certain type out there that thinks they have a God-given right to a life without any inconveniences or, barring that, unanticipated expenses. Sometimes, after an inspector's complete paperwork and diligent efforts to explain a house's existing problems, a buyer might decide the shit he signed off on is not actually okay with him. This buyer might turn out to be both impulsive *and* a dick, always a bad combination.

So, this hypothetical buyer jumps in with both feet, and when minor issues turned into expensive headaches, he can't possibly imagine how fixing the problem he knew his house had when he bought it could possibly be his responsibility. He wants someone else – maybe someone who makes like a quarter of his annual income – to cover the bill because if there's one thing he knows about the universe it's that nothing is ever his responsibility.

That shit was out there. The danger was real. Pete, however, knew how to protect himself. He did a good job, he documented like a motherfucker, he verbally confirmed everything of note, and he made sure the paper trail always covered his ass. He figured that if you can't avoid getting sued, you can keep those suits from becoming real problems.

That was exactly how Pete had operated his entire career. Except once. He'd been inspecting a McMansion in Olmos Park, not five years old, and found some significant structural damage with the roof. Nothing was about to cave in, but the house was going to need work in the next year or two, which was outrageous for a structure so new. The realtor, Candi Watson, had obviously known about it, because she'd stood on the lawn watching him while he climbed around up there, and she cornered him as soon as he'd come down. Candi was one of the big movers in these old San Antonio neighborhoods, and she sent a lot of business Pete's way. A brittle woman in her early sixties, bleach blonde, impeccably dressed, and affluently gaunt, Candi treated Pete with the same condescending reserve she probably used on her maid and valet parkers, but she was a lucrative contact, and he'd always been content to kiss her ass.

"Listen," she'd said to him, resting her fingertips momentarily against his upper arm. Pete was pretty sure it was the first time in their ten years of business that she'd ever touched him. "These people are *impossible*. I've shown them two dozen places, and they've turned everything down for the most absurd reasons. They like this one, and they're leaning toward it, but I know them, and if your report spooks them, they'll walk. All homes are going to need some work. You know that. And they can afford it." All the while she spoke, she was reaching into her purse, but the look on her face said she had no idea what her hand could possibly be up to. Finally she pulled out an envelope and tucked it into the creases of Pete's folded arms. "The roof is just fine."

Pete grabbed the envelope with his fingertips, uncrossed his arms, and peeked inside just long enough to see that it was thick with $50s. The look on Candi's face suggested that looking had been disturbingly crass.

Pete tried to hand the envelope back to her. "Candi, I appreciate your position, but you know I can't—"

She refused to take it, taking a step back and holding up her hands like Pete was about to do something unsavory. "How much business have I sent your way over the years?"

"And I appreciate that, but this could ruin me."

"It won't ruin you," she said, laughing like he'd suggested she could get pregnant from a toilet seat. "You'll never hear a squeak about this, and if you do, I promise to make it go away. Your reputation will be protected, and you won't be out one cent in legal fees. If this blows up in our faces, I can take care of it and still come out ahead. Everyone wins, Pete, including the client. You're in a service industry. So, serve."

When he didn't say anything, she said, "That's five thousand dollars in there. Don't tell me you can't use it."

Pete had taken the money, less, he would later think, because he wanted it than because there was nothing else to do with it other than drop it on the ground or shove it inside Candi's silk blouse. He had known at that moment that he could either walk away with some extra cash or walk away without one of his best business generators. There had been no third choice.

Six months later, when the buyers sued him, Pete had immediately tried to contact Candi, but she refused to take his calls. More than that, she began to talk about him to other realtors and inspectors. She'd been worried about him for a long time. Pete was sloppy, she said. He was lazy. Was it incompetence or negligence, she wondered? Had that been beer she'd smelled on his breath during that inspection a few weeks back? Even so, with all her doubts about him, she was scandalized that he could botch an inspection so badly.

Pete's work began to dry up. Now he was lucky to get one or two inspections a week, and he had a deposition coming up in which he had no choice but to lie or condemn himself. But lying, he knew, was only delaying the inevitable since he'd signed his name to a bad inspection, and the homeowners could prove it. They were asking for $50,000 to replace the roof and cover water damages. The amount was outrageous unless they were planning on using gold tiles, but his lawyer said they wouldn't get more than $25,000. Even so, a settlement like that would mean bankruptcy and the end of Pete's livelihood. He owned his house, but he'd be unable to pay his property taxes. He was pretty much looking at his life blowing up in his face.

On Monday morning, with nothing else to do with his time, Pete drove over to the Home Depot parking lot and checked his phone which, typical for these days, had no messages. He made some phone calls he suspected would be pointless. Only the most marginal and poorly connected realtors hadn't heard that Pete was bad news. Still, he kept trying because what the hell else was he going to do.

After he'd exhausted all his follow-ups, Pete tried Candi's office one more time. Why not? Maybe she'd had a chance to reflect. Maybe he could catch her in a good mood. But no luck. Her receptionist was very apologetic. Candi was not in right now. Would he care to leave a voicemail? Pete would not, and there was no point trying her cell phone. She rejected all his calls. Once, when he'd tried to call from a different phone, she'd disconnected the second she heard his voice.

Maybe he should go get a beer.Why the hell not? Sitting in a bar and watching ESPN all day sure sounded a whole lot better than sitting in his truck. If he was going to do nothing, it might as well be enjoyable.

He was on the verge of having talked himself into it. His fingers were on the keys, and he was ready to twist, but then he stopped himself. What the hell was he doing? Was he really going to turn into a drunk because life had knocked him down and was repeatedly kicking him in the balls? How had he allowed this to happen? Everyone walked all over him, and he did nothing to stop it. Well, fuck that, he decided. He'd turn into a drunk if he ran out of options. The barstool would always be waiting for him. For now, it was time to push back a little.

He hated to say it, but he needed to take a page from Douchebag William's book of douchebaggery. He couldn't make himself younger or have more hair, and while getting back into shape was a good idea, he couldn't take care of that at this exact moment. None of that mattered, though. Douchebag William didn't shoulder his way through life because of his looks. They helped, sure, but it was his attitude. Maybe his looks were why he had the attitude in the first place, but to be a first class dick like the Douche, all you really needed was to act like the world was going to bend to your will whether it wanted to or not.

It was time for Pete to take action instead of waiting for everyone to stop walking all over him. He had to deal with Jenny's crummy attitude, and he had to get Candi to step up and do what she'd said she would, but first things first. He had an idea, a way to push back, and it was going to make him feel good, so that's where he was going to start.

Pete picked up the phone and called his old high school friend, Grant McNabb. Grant was a private investigator, which was apparently a lot less exciting than it appeared on TV. Mostly he sat in an office and conducted interviews and looked things up on the computer. He had some guys who worked for him who would sit in cars and try to snap pictures of assholes cheating on their wives, but Grant said that work was boring as hell. He preferred to hang out at his desk, eating potato chips, and occasionally watching porn.

Grant listened to a sanitized version of Pete's story. There was a neighbor across the street who was giving Pete attitude. It would be helpful to know something about the guy before pushing back.

"That's not a problem," Grant said. "No charge, but next time we hang, beers are on you."

"Deal." It felt good. You ask for something, and you get it. That's all it takes.

"It shouldn't be too hard," Grant said. "Let me hit you up in a few hours."

Feeling like he was being forceful, getting stuff done, Pete turned on the truck and drove over to Candi Watson's office on Broadway. As a realtor, she was obviously out much of the day, but the office was still her home base, and Pete knew she had to check in once in a while.

Since she had first refused to honor her promise, Pete had thought about going to confront her. Just about every day he'd imagined what it would be like to go to her office, lean over her while she cringed and promised to make good. He hadn't done it because it was the nuclear option. If she didn't give in, he would never be able to back track and hope for a resolution, so he kept putting it off. The encounter with Douchebag William had made it clear, however, that no one was going to treat him with respect or take him seriously if he didn't demand it.

Pete parked his truck outside her office, right next to Candi's BMW. He took two spaces, just to show he knew how to be as much of a dick as the next guy, and then he walked into the reception area, just in time to see the door to Candi's office close. Behind the front desk, a plump redheaded woman was working the phones.

"Can I help you?" she asked. Her nervous expression suggested she knew exactly who he was and what he wanted. Candi was hiding in her office and had thrown the receptionist to the wolves.

That's what Pete was now, he told himself. The wolves.

"I'd like to talk to Candi," he said, trying to keep his voice somewhere between badass and polite. He was going for resolute.

"I'm afraid she'd not here," the receptionist attempted.

"Huh," Pete said. "That's funny, because her car is right outside, and I just saw her close her door."

The woman shook her head, looking like she was on the verge of tears. "She's not here."

Pete moved to walk toward Candi's office. "I'll just have a peek."

The woman rose up and blocked him. There was no way he was going to be able to open the door to her office without touching her, and Pete understood that would be a mistake. Accidentally brush one of her big tits and she'd be crying rape, so he took a few steps back, palms up to show there was no titty-touching scheduled into his calendar.

"I'll just wait for her." Pete lowered himself into one of the chairs lining the wall.

"She won't be coming in at all today." The words were ordinary, but the tone suggested she was pleading for her life with a bankrobber.

Pete felt his heart pounding. He was a little nervous himself, but this woman didn't know that, and she was taking him seriously. He liked that.

"Please," she said to him. "There's no point in waiting."

"You know what," Pete said. "It turns out that I have nothing else to do, so I don't mind."

She sat down at her desk and leveled her gaze at him. After taking a deep breath she said, "I'm afraid I'm going to have to ask you to leave."

Pete smiled and shrugged, but did not reply. He picked up a copy of *Texas Highways* magazine, turned a few pages and looked at the pictures with great interest, as though the magazine had some kind of purpose other than to take up space in waiting rooms. After a few seconds, he peeked up to watch the heavy woman nervously answer the phone, her eyes wide, her hands unsteady as she took messages. She asked people to repeat things. She dropped pens. Pete liked that she was having a hard time concentrating. That, he thought, is what happens when you fuck with me. He would have liked the world's response to his wrath to be a little more significant than botched phone messages, but it was a start.

After almost an hour, with no sign of Candi emerging from the shelter of her office, Pete saw a police car pull into the parking lot, its lights flashing to signal its seriousness. Pete felt an electric jolt of fear pass through him, but he told himself that he would be fine. He had done nothing wrong. This was a reception area, open to the public, and he was waiting for the person who worked in this office, a person with whom he had legitimate business.

The policeman, a baby-faced guy in his mid-20s, came into the reception area, his radio squawking. He looked at the receptionist, but didn't say anything to her. Instead, he turned to Pete, and squinted with disdain, as if he already knew everything he needed to know.

"Sir," he said. "We have a report that you are being disruptive."

"That's not true," Pete said calmly. "I'm waiting to talk to Candi Watson. This is where she works, and I have business with her. I'm just sitting here quietly until she's free."

"Sir," the policeman said with distracted and immensely insincere politeness, "it's my understanding that you've been informed that Miss Watson is not in."

Pete smiled. "I'm hoping she'll stop by."

"Sir, have you been asked to leave?"

"Yes, but for no good reason. I need to speak to Candi Watson, and this is her office. No one has explained to me why I can't wait here."

"Sir, this is private business, and if the employees have asked you to leave, you are obligated to do so."

Pete stood because he didn't like the cop looking down at him. He rose slowly, however, and kept his hands visible, so there would be no misunderstandings. "Look, officer, I get that, but I want to talk to Candi Watson on a matter of business. Her office is right there, and she's inside it. She refuses to take my calls. She won't see me. I haven't threatened her or anyone else. If you want to hang out here while we talk, that's just fine with me. You can arrest me if I do anything illegal."

"Sir," the policeman said, "please don't tell me how to exercise my duties."

"I'm not telling you anything," Pete said, his voice growing just the tiniest bit louder.

"Sir, please do not raise your voice. I understand that you think you have business here, but that's not my concern. My concern is that you have been asked to vacate private property, and you are refusing to do so. If you continue to refuse, I'm going to have to detain you."

"Detain me?" Pete asked. "So, that means... what? I'll be in detention?"

"Sir," the policeman said, "I am going to have to give you your final warning."

The policeman leveled his apathetic gaze at him, and Pete knew he was on thin ice now. If he didn't eat this cop's shit, like he had to eat everyone else's shit, he would be cuffed. Pete had to walk out of there, humiliated and helpless, or go to jail, maybe get tased or pepper sprayed or some bullshit like that. Fuck it, he thought. Let them fucking detain me. For what? For sitting in a waiting room? Let's see how those charges stand up in court. Good luck with that. Make all the threats you want, he decided, I'm standing my ground.

But he walked out. He knew he couldn't bear to explain all of this to Jenny and Addison. He couldn't deal with yet one more disaster, so he took the shame of defeat instead. Without looking at the receptionist, he walked out and got into his truck.

He sat behind the wheel and watched while the cop talked to the receptionist. He said something and smiled. The receptionist laughed and twirled her red hair around a finger. Pete pulled out of his parking spot and went back to the Home Depot, where he sat for several hours.

* * *

Later that afternoon, Grant returned his call.

"Your guy's a lawyer," Grant said.

"Big surprise."

"Yeah. Not married, no kids. Works at a firm downtown doing some kind of financial bullshit I can't understand. No history of legal problems. He looks pretty clean."

Pete grabbed his clipboard and wrote down the name and address of the firm. "What time does he usually get off work?"

"Hold on," Grant said, and the sound of fingers on a computer keyboard came over the line. "My behavior prediction algorithm says he'll leave his office today between 5:15 and 5:21."

"Really?"

"Fuck, no," Grant said. "You think life is like a TV show where a guy with a computer can find out what you had for dinner last Wednesday?"

Pete sighed. "Thanks, man. I owe you."

Okay, so Grant didn't know what time he got out exactly, but Pete figured it would not be before 5:00, so he put his truck in gear and headed downtown. A guy like that, with no family, wouldn't necessarily be out the door early, but Pete decided to take a chance. Better to catch him off guard, to see that Pete was not a guy to be fucking with.

He made it downtown just before five and was lucky enough to find a spot on Commerce just across the street from the Douche's office. He sat there and waited. Fifteen minutes later, he saw why Grant hired out guys to do the legwork. It was boring as shit. He decided he would give it until six and then call it a day.

Then, there he was, coming out of his office in a fancy suit, with a leather briefcase in his hand, like he was some sort of a big shot. He was walking with a woman, a real looker too. She wore a skirt suit, the sort of thing Pete usually found unattractive, but this one made it work. She had shoulder length dark hair and gigantic brown eyes, and a killer body. Her skin was a very light brown, so she was probably a Mexican – also the sort of thing that Pete didn't usually go for, but this girl was radiant, and she pulled off the Latina thing no problem.

This is a stupid idea, Pete decided. He had to be out of his mind to even be thinking about this. He pressed himself back into his seat so his neighbor wouldn't catch a glimpse of him, which was kind of a stupid thing to do since his name and number were on the side of his truck.

In fact, Douchebag William glanced over. Pete realized he'd been spotted. Maybe he could play it off as a coincidence, but probably not. He was going to look like a creepy stalker now. Well, fuck that. Fate wasn't going to let him chicken out, so he sucked in a big gulp of air, reminded himself that he was king shit, and he wasn't going to get pushed around by anyone. Then he opened the door, dodged traffic to cross the street, and planted himself directly across from William.

"Hey there, neighbor," he said in that way he had that sounded sort of friendly but was really meant to be menacing.

William and the woman stopped. The woman actually had a disgusted look on her face, like Pete was a homeless guy or something.

William let the seconds tick by, staring but not saying anything, so Pete decided to pick up the slack. "You and your sister out for a stroll?" He figured if the Douche could accuse him of being a Mexican, Pete could return the favor.

"Do you want something?" William set his jaw, planted his feet, trying to act all touch guy.

"Just wanted to say hello," Pete said. "Since we're neighbors and all."

The thing was, Pete wasn't entirely sure what he wanted now that he was here. Maybe he'd been hoping that William would be all freaked out seeing him here – the whole *I know where you work* thing – but it didn't seem to impress him. In fact, now that he was here, Pete had to work hard not to let his doubt and embarrassment show.

"William, let's go," the woman said, all agitated, like Pete was going to rape her or something.

"No, it's cool," William said, his voice neutral, almost cold. "Pete is my neighbor." He turned to Pete. "You look a little agitated, Pete. You have a rough day?"

"Yeah, well that's how it goes in my line of work."

William looked across the street to Pete's truck, eying the sign on the side. "Home inspections, huh?"

"That's right," Pete said.

"I've seen the truck in your driveway."

Now he was expecting the usual crap: Can you check to see if we need more insulation; should I replace my pipes; how out of date is my wiring. All that bullshit.

"Nice," William said. "Look, I shouldn't have given you such a hard time the other day. You caught me in the middle of something. I get the whole lawn thing from your point of view, and I realize you don't get it from mine. So, maybe you should."

Now Pete was thrown. William was suddenly being all reasonable. That would be fine if he were backing down, maybe worried that Pete knew about the headless goat in the backyard, but that wasn't it. He wasn't giving an inch of turf. Pete recognized exactly what was going in. William was being *magnanimous*. He was *condescending* to be nice to his blue collar neighbor. It was a smart move, because now Pete couldn't escalate things without looking like a dick, but if he didn't, then he would be a pussy.

Pete was seething, but still, he had to admire it. The guy had moves. He knew how to be tough in front of the hot Mexican girl without getting into a scrap and looking like an asshole.

"Maybe I should what?" Pete finally said.

"Maybe you should know what it's all about." He cracked the thinnest of smiles. "I like your attitude. A guy like you would fit right in."

Now he was sure the Douche was making fun of him. "What would I be fitting in with?"

"You'll see. Come on by my place tomorrow night at eleven. I know it's late, but that's what time we get started."

"Started with what?" Pete asked.

"Mowing the lawn."

* * *

Though he told himself a dozen times over he wasn't going to do it, that he didn't want any part of his asshole neighbor or his goat-draining religion, Pete ended up wandering over to William's house at a quarter after eleven. There were cars parked up and down the street, and lights on at the house, but no noise escaped onto the stoop when Pete rang the bell.

William opened the door, wearing his casual jeans and t-shirt combo. This did not surprise him. What surprised him were the William clones milling around the house, all of them fit, all of them wearing jeans and tight t-shirts. Some of the shirts named out-of-state schools, but most of the single-colored shirts were black. They stood in small groups, and each guy who was talking was acting like what he had to say was the most interesting thing anyone had ever uttered in the history of assholes shooting off their mouths. Most of them had goblets of red wine, though a few guys were doing shots of tequila they poured out of a weirdly-shaped bottle.

William waved Pete inside, putting a hand on his shoulder as he quickly closed the door behind him. William ushered Pete inside the room, pressing him forward a little too forcefully for Pete's comfort.

"Listen up, guys," William announced.

The men ceased their conversation. They looked up from their drinks and important conversations and hilarious stories. They pointed their square jaws in his direction. Pete, who had once exuded his own feral confidence now felt like the basset hound among the wolves. He felt old and fat and bald, and he wished to hell he were somewhere else.

"This is Pete," William announced. "He lives across the street, and he came by over the weekend to *request* I cut my lawn."

The GQ set burst into cruel laughter.

Pete wanted to get the hell out of there. He wanted to run. He was actually afraid, afraid of the other guys, of getting beaten up. He suddenly had the feeling that it was going to be him out back, dangling from the scaffolding, his blood dripping into a metal bucket. It was going to be his head propped on a department store manikin. That's why he'd been invited. He was the human sacrifice for their fucked up devil-worshiping religion, and Pete had walked right into it. He might as well have been wearing a shirt that pronounced ASK ME ABOUT BEING A SACRIFICE TO SATAN. It was ridiculous and impossible and depressing, but it was all undeniably true. But even more than he was afraid of staying, he was afraid of leaving, of being a total fucking coward who ran in terror from Douchebag William's house. That was why he stayed put.

William raised his hand good naturedly, like a politician on a stump speech after enumerating the wrong-headed ideas of the opponent. "I know. I know. I thought the same thing too. Pussy. Fat, old, bald guy comes to *my* house telling me what to do with *my* lawn? Give me a break, right?"

There were murmurs of agreement. And more laughter. They were laughing at Pete, and that was fucking bullshit. He'd been feeling old just a second ago, but that was his feeling, and he had the right to it. He didn't have more than ten years on most of these guys, so maybe they should all just shut the fuck up.

Pete opened his mouth to explain to them the wisdom of doing exactly that. He was going to tell Douchebag William and his goblet-fondling metrosexual friends to fuck the hell off, but the thing was, he couldn't speak. He felt as though he'd lost control of his throat muscles. He could breath, but no sounds were coming out. It was like one of those dreams where you try to scream but you can't, except that this was real life, and there were a dozen alpha males standing around him, drinking expensive wine and staring at him, amused, while his eyes bulged.

"But the thing is," William continued, "he then showed up at my place of work. He found out where my office was, and he waited outside, and when I came out with a babe on my arm, he confronted me. He got in my face. He *menaced* me. In *public*."

Pete braced himself for more jeers, for more laughter and pointing and humiliation, but that's not what happened. The Sunday-*New-York-Times*-readers weren't jeering or smiling anymore. They were nodding at him, lips pressed together in approval. One guy took a big sip of wine and said, "Nice," and his saying it was like a wizard waving a wand. The muscles in Pete's throat relaxed. He knew he could speak, but he didn't want to. He felt like he wanted to listen.

"Yeah," William agreed. "That's what I thought. I said to myself, here's a guy with a, a huge sack. Here's a guy who doesn't put up with someone fucking with him. Here's a guy who is one of us."

The rest of the guys were nodding vigorously now. Some of them were raising their glasses to toast him.

Pete now decided it was time to exercise his restored powers of speech. "One of you what?"

William waved at one of the guys, who brought them both goblets of wine. "Couldn't hurt to have a drink while I explain it."

Pete looked at the glass a little warily. He'd drink wine if he had to. It beat staying sober, especially at times like this, but he never much liked it. "Any chance I could get a beer."

William laughed, like Pete was a kid who said he wanted to be a space pirate when he grew up. "No, man, you can't drink that garbage if you want to hang with us. That's what I'm trying to tell you. Me and the guys, we're turning back the clock." He raised his glass in salute. "You know what happened to the Neanderthals, Pete?"

"How the fuck should I know that?" he asked, quite reasonably he believed.

"People used to think our ancestors wiped them out, that we outfought them. Turns out that isn't true. People today have around two percent Neanderthal DNA, which means we didn't outfight them, we outfucked them. We interbred them out of existence. But that also means we're them. We're still cavemen. We have that within us. All of us here do HyperStrong. You ever heard of that?"

Pete knew a couple of guys, contractors, who did HyperStrong. It was this crazy workout cult that was supposed to kick your ass. You had to join a special gym, which cost like $300 a month, and you could only go for scheduled classes where you would climb ropes and hit big tires with sledgehammers. It sounded like bullshit to Pete, but the guys he knew who did it were in great shape and they swore by it. Exercise classes never much appealed to Pete. He didn't care how macho the equipment was, it still smacked of jazzercize. When he went to the gym, which he was meaning to start doing again real soon, he liked to lift on his own schedule, not when some dick with a stopwatch blew a whistle at him.

Most of these opinions he kept to himself, however. "Yeah, I've heard of it."

"We do the paleo diet, too. You ever hear of that?"

Pete shook his head.

"We eat only what cavemen ate. Meat – what we hunt ourselves or grass-fed beef, not that factory-farmed bullshit, which is full of antibiotics and hormones. Organic fruits and vegetables, and that's it. No grains. No beans. No packaged foods. No beer. No booze at all except wine and tequila."

"Jesus," said Pete, who did not think a life without Big Macs and cold brews was worth living. "No wonder the cavemen went extinct."

"There's a period of adjustment," William agreed, "but then you know what you feel?"

"Like you want to order a pizza?" Pete asked.

"You feel strong. You feel fit. You feel like a man, Pete. When was the last time you felt like a real man?"

Pete opened his mouth to object, but he saw these guys staring at him, all of them with their perfect bods and chiseled good looks.

"We weren't always this fit," William said. "I used to weigh 250 pounds. I was a lardass, and I couldn't get a girl to save my life. Look at me now."

"And you became a real man because you exercised and changed what you ate?" Pete asked.

"That's just two of the three things," William said.

Pete sensed he was supposed to ask, and he hated to be made to perform like a monkey, but he had to know. "What was the third?"

"Our religion."

Pete looked William in the eye. He weighed too much because he drank too much beer and ate too much crap, but so the hell what? He was an American, and he could do what the fuck he wanted. He was not going to let this guy intimidate him with his cult bullshit.

"Is that the religion that doesn't let you cut your lawn but does let you hang a headless goat in your backyard?"

William met his gaze and grinned. "That's the one."

* * *

They were sitting in a dark room. It was upstairs, and it seemed to have been designed for this exact purpose, for rituals. There were benches along the wall, and a fire pit right in the center of the floor, with a chimney opened above it. There was an altar of some kind, too, made of pale rock, on which sat a stone bowl, like the kind they use to make guacamole at your table in fancy Mexican restaurants. Next to it stood the manikin, the one he'd seen outside. It still had the goat head propped on its neck.

Their religion was like their diet, William had explained while they were still downstairs. It was paleo. It turned out they weren't Satanists, they were animists, and they summoned and commanded and served – not worshipped – the spirits of things. Everything has a spirit, William said. Plants and animals, and even mechanical things, like cars and computers. He didn't know why – if they had them naturally, the way people had souls, or if spirits attached themselves to things and took on characteristics of the new home. Both theories were much debated in animist circles, but William made it clear that he really didn't give a shit either way. He didn't know how his cell phone worked either. The why wasn't important. What mattered was that you could make these spirits work for you.

"That's why I've been letting my lawn grow," William explained. "I've been cultivating its spirit."

"The lawn has a spirit?" Pete repeated.

"That's right."

"So, why don't the, like, blades of grass each have their own spirit?"

A couple of the guys murmured. "That's a really good question," one said.

"He's like a professor or something," said another.

"We don't really know the answer to that," William said. "As near as I can tell, it's because we think of the lawn as one thing, rather than paying attention to each blade of grass, and somehow humans will play a role here. The point is that we cultivate the spirit of the lawn, we feed it by letting the lawn grow, we pay homage to it, and then we sacrifice its physical form. In so doing, we take on the properties of that spirit and bring them into our lives. In this case, growth, fecundity, abundance."

"That's fucking bullshit," Pete opined.

William smiled.

Pete might have walked out, but he didn't. Instead, when William announced it was time, he walked upstairs with the others. They sat by the fire in the dark, and they chanted *Lawn, Lawn, Lawn,* over and over again. Each of them took turns throwing a handful of grass into the flames. When they had done this for a good hour, William stood and said, "Who shall make the sacrifice and reap the greatest share of the spirit's blessings?"

One of the men said, "Let it be our new brother!" They all pointed and chanted *Pete, Pete, Pete.*

William beckoned him forward, and Pete stood by the fire. William handed him a handful of grass, and Pete threw it onto the flames. Then William put his hand in a stone bowl, and it came out dark and dripping. In the flickering light, Pete could see the hand was covered with blood, and he had no doubt it was the blood from the sacrificed goat.

William smeared some of the blood on Pete's head, but most of his attention was given to the images he made on the altar, using his finger to paint with blood. He made three designs, like spiraling circles, and then, in the center of them, he pressed his hand, dripping with blood, to make a print.

"The powers that surround us have been summoned," William said. "They attend us. Let us destroy what we have created in homage to them. Our brother Pete will have the honor."

That was how, at two in the morning, Pete ended up outside William's house, mowing the lawn with an old fashioned hand-push mower. Sweat poured down his back while inside the house the HyperStrong crew drank wine and, he was sure, laughed at him. He knew he ought to throw down the mower and walk away. He was being made fun of, made a fool of, but he kept mowing all the same until the grass was shorn and Pete was exhausted and resentful.

Angry and humiliated, ready to fight one of them – or all of them – Pete walked through the front door. His clothes were dripping with sweat. His eyes stung and his muscles ached. William and his friends looked at him, but they did not laugh. They raised their goblets of wine in a toast, and somehow that simple gesture seemed to drain Pete of all his anger.

"I think you're really going to like what happens next," William said.

"What's going to happen?" Pete asked.

"Growth."

* * *

Back in his own house, Pete slipped through the darkness to the refrigerator. It was almost three in the morning, and all was quiet. He took out a beer, pulled the tab from the can and sank back in the kitchen chair. He didn't give a crap that beer was made from grains and wasn't what some hooting Neanderthal would drink. They didn't drink it because they didn't have it. If someone had offered a thirsty caveman a can of beer, he'd drink the shit out of it. That was what Pete did.

He still felt the slight buzz of shame. How had he participated in that completely gay ritual, and let an asshole smear him with goat blood? That was bad enough, but how had he allowed himself to be talked into mowing the lawn? He would have been sure that William and his friend were mocking him, except they'd seemed so damn serious about it all. After he'd left, he'd even pressed his ear to the front door, expecting to hear the sound of uproarious laughter, but there had only been solemn murmurings. If it had not all been a practical joke, then it meant that they had been serious about the whole thing, and maybe that was even worse.

He finished his beer and tore open another and sat in the dark, still catching his breath and cooling off. In the distance, he listened to the dog slinking along the wooden floors, its nails clicking with each step. Only after he'd thrown away his third can of beer, undressed, and climbed into bed did he remember that the dog had been dead for more than a year.

* * *

Jenny was furious. Pete had tracked grass all through the house, and the sheets were strained with streaks of green and there was something brown on the pillow. "What the hell were you doing?" she demanded, but walked out of the bedroom before Pete could answer. The answer, he realized, wasn't the point. Demanding an answer was the point.

Pete sat at the breakfast table with Addison. Jenny was too angry at having had to sweep grass off the floor to bring herself to join them. Addison, as usual, made a fuss about having to eat breakfast, and did a lot of sighing over her cereal.

"Come on," Pete told her. "Eat something. You don't want to be hungry all day."

She looked up at him, like she was ready to flash one of her looks of exasperation, to roll her eyes and shoot daggers with her eyes.

He'd become jumpy at the prospect of talking to his own daughter. Anything might set her off. He knew it was just a part of growing up, but she used to be his little girl. He used to take her to the park and to Missions games, and now she looked at him as though he were the most embarrassing thing in the world. He wanted her to be sweet again.

He braced himself for that look now, but when she met his eye she paused, like she saw something she hadn't expected.

"Okay," she said. And she ate.

A half an hour later, Pete had pulled into the Home Depot parking lot where he could make calls and try to drum up business. When he turned on his work phone, there were nearly a dozen messages waiting for him, and he knew that couldn't be good. Obviously, something had blown up with his lawsuit, and he cringed as he punched in his code to hear his messages.

It was a mix of call backs and follow-up requests, but there were also three requests for inspections. Three in one morning. That had happened before, but not since the lawsuit. Not since things had started to go bad for him. Maybe it was a coincidence, or maybe there really was something to all this paleo stuff.

The idea seemed laughable. A bunch of rich assholes chanted and made a few designs in goat blood, and after a good lawn-mowing Pete gets his wishes granted. It was too stupid to consider seriously, but, on the other hand, it also seemed to be true. Things were going his way, and all at once. Pete was a skeptic, and proud of it, but he had to admit this didn't look like a coincidence.

And then there was the dog, Howard. It had really been Jenny's dog – a big, slobbering golden lab. Pete had walked it and fed it and done all the things he was supposed to do, but he'd never been an animal person, and his relationship had never moved much beyond toleration. When it died, Jenny and Addison both cried their eyes out, but Pete had mostly felt relief.

He'd heard the dog last night. He was sure of it. He hadn't been drunk, and being tired wouldn't have made him imagine what wasn't there. Now that he thought about it, the memory of the dog was clear and precise. He'd fallen asleep thinking that he hoped the fucking thing didn't wake him.

Not that Pete believed in ghost dogs any more than he believed in caveman spirits. But still, it was kind of strange. Maybe it was even a little spooky, but in the light of day, in his truck, with jobs waiting on him, it was easy to push those thoughts aside.

Pete began returning calls furiously, and was able to set up an appointment for the late morning, and two for the afternoon. The rest of the week was already starting to fill up. This didn't really solve his problems, of course. He still had the lawsuit to deal with, and he was going to lose that. When he did, he'd be screwed, and caveman mojo was not going to make things any better. Even so, income was better than no income. He couldn't control the future, so he had to live in the now.

When he got home, he was covered with sweat and grime. It made him realize how much faking it these past few weeks should have been obvious to anyone paying attention. The first thing he had to do was shower, and as he was washing himself off, he was surprised, and not at all displeased, to see that he was sporting a massive, spontaneous boner. This kind of thing didn't happen all that often anymore, and given that he hadn't been working up any nasty ideas in his head, it was pretty much completely unexpected. He felt big, like maybe this was a bigger boner than he'd ever had before. Did this paleo crap worked like those pills you saw advertised on the internet? Anything, it seemed to him, was possible.

As he changed into a clean t-shirt and jeans, Pete couldn't help but think that it had been way too long since he'd given Jenny some action in the sack. Maybe that's what she needed. The more he thought about it, the more that made sense. She'd been down on him because his sex drive had been off, which was only natural since he'd been so worried about money. Now there was work, which wasn't the same as the lawsuit going away, but it sure felt like things were turning around. A full schedule of inspections was all he needed to feel confident. He knew exactly what he had to do to get his marriage back on track.

During dinner he caught himself leering at Jenny, and a couple of times she asked him if he was feeling okay or if he had something in his eye. Addison, who was apparently more perceptive than her mother, turned away with a blush. Well, so what? He wasn't ashamed of finding his wife attractive, and it was good for kids to see their parents behaving affectionately.

After dinner, Addison went off to her room to scroll endlessly on her phone. When Jenny had finished cleaning up, Pete put an arm around her and gave her a kiss on the cheek. "What do you say the two of us go upstairs and take care of some business?" He put a hand on her back and let it drift downward.

Jenny shoved him away. "What are you doing?" She looked at him like he'd just shoved a dildo up her ass, which had not occurred to him until that moment, but now that he thought about it, he kind of liked the idea.

"What do you think I'm doing?" he asked, still trying to sound seductive, but he knew a little bit of his defensiveness was getting through. He had expected her to respond a little more warmly, not rebuke him.

"It's 7:30!" Jenny shouted at him, like this was the single most damning indictment in the history of human depravity. Better he should have tossed a bag full of severed infant heads on the floor than touched her ass before eight.

"So what?" It wasn't like they'd never had sex before bedtime before, though, admittedly, it had been a while since that had happened.

"I'm just, I don't know," she said, waving her hands around, now acting more confused than angry, like she was trying to recast her reaction. "You just took me by surprise is all."

"Okay, then," he said, "well, now that the surprise is over—"

"Forget it," she said. "I'm not in the mood *now*. Not after *that*."

"You're not in the mood because I suggested we go upstairs?" Pete asked, his voice sounding sharp.

"Not when you take that tone with me" Jenny said.

"I didn't take that tone before you started acting this way."

"That," she said, "is a lie. I don't like to be lied to." She leveled her gaze at him until it was absolutely clear that she had been injured and no ordinary apology was going to make this wound heal. She stared at him until he turned away.

Pete wandered into the living room and stood, momentarily dazed, his boner a distant, and inexplicably shameful, memory. Through the fog of confusion, disappointment, embarrassment, and anger, he could see no way forward that did not involve beer. He risked a snatch and grab in the kitchen for a can, and was ready to pry one loose. Then, thinking better of it, planning for the future, committing to a course of action, he grabbed the whole six and stormed out of the house.

He wanted Jenny to wonder where he'd gone off to, to worry about him, to fear that he had things going on, interesting things, that would leave her behind. He probably ought to get into his truck and go drive somewhere to drink his six pack, but he didn't have the energy for it, not after working all day. So he sat down on the porch swing and popped the first can.

He was working on popping the fourth can when he saw William's car pull into the circular driveway. When his neighbor emerged from his car, Pete gave him a wave with his beer. William began to walk over.

He wore a dark suit that, even in the dim glow of the porch light, Pete could tell was expertly tailored, showing off broad shoulders and a trim waist. The shirt was slightly wrinkled and a little bit untucked, affecting the kind of unkempt macho appearance of a magazine ad.

"What's up?" Pete asked. "Beer?"

"I don't drink beer," William said, maybe a little sternly. "I told you that. You shouldn't either."

"Shit, I'm celebrating. Business picked up this morning."

William nodded. Maybe a little bit of a smile crept up the corners of his mouth. It wasn't the smile of someone who was happy for someone else's success. It was the smile of a guy who has been proven right. "I told you what we do works. That's why you should knock that off." He gestured toward the beer. "It's not paleo."

Pete waved his hand. "Come on. It's not like I joined a monastery or something."

"No, it's not," agreed William, "because monks drink beer. We don't." He looked at the swing like he considered sitting, but he likely decided it was too small, and sitting would be kind of gay. "You behave according to the rules of our tribe."

"That's pretty strict, don't you think?"

"It's the way it works," William said. "Living like our ancestors is what grants us the power of our ancestors, dude. That's the deal. You think I don't like beer? You think, if we are just going on taste, I wouldn't go for a Trappist Dubbel over a Châteauneuf-du-Pape?"

Pete, who suddenly had no idea what was being discussed, decided to say nothing.

"You can't get something for nothing, brah," William said. "What we're talking about, is getting a whole lot for relatively little. You have to make a few sacrifices, sure, but those sacrifices make you healthier, so it's really not such a bad thing."

"I guess," Pete agreed uncomfortably. He wanted to take another sip of beer, but thought maybe that would be the liquid equivalent of giving William the finger.

"Tell you what?" William said. "Why don't you come to one of our HyperStrong classes? You're not going to believe how good you feel after."

"Group exercise isn't really my thing," Pete said, feeling the flab in his arms and the softness in his belly like they were throbbing. He didn't want William and his friends to see how out of shape he was or how much more they could lift than he could.

"You want to keep reaping the rewards of last night, right?" William said. Without waiting for an answer, he continued. "Just come to the class. You'll see." He took a pen and a piece of paper from his jacket pocket and wrote something down then handed it to Pete. "Be there," he said, and it was not a request.

* * *

To know Pete, Pete believed, was to know that he did not like to be told what to do, so he had been completely prepared to crumple up, throw away, and possibly even flush the piece of paper William had given him. The chances that he would piss on it first were pretty high. He did not do any of that, however. Instead, he set it aside, because he liked to think that people also knew he was a thinker. Pete was a thinking man, and a thinking man liked to keep his options open.

So the next day, still stinging from Jenny's rejection, Pete had to face a few more disappointments. At breakfast, Addison was back to being her usual sullen self, and while there were a few calls waiting for him on his voicemail, there were fewer than the day before, and a couple of cancellations as well. The paleo magic, it seemed, was fading, and rather than sticking to his guns and living by his principles, Pete knew it was maybe time to get back

Paleo

in the good graces of Douchebag William and his clan of the cave dicks.

Accordingly, Pete swung by the house, changed into his gym clothes, which smelled of the drawer they'd been sitting in, untouched, for two years, and headed over to Iron Grip HyperStrong Fitness and Lifestyle Studio, located in a former furniture store that had gone bankrupt. The building had sat empty for quite some time, but now it was full of weights and racks and bars, straps dangling from the ceiling, gigantic tires, sledgehammers, and fifty foot ropes as thick as Pete's arm.

He showed up a few minutes early, and found Pete chatting up a woman, tan and blonde, as fit as a protein powder model. When Pete walked in, he immediately turned away from the woman and clapped Pete on the back.

"Great to see you here, brah. You are going to love it."

Pete looked around dubiously, taking in the twenty five or so people, all at least ten years younger than he was, all incredibly fit. They moved with ease around equipment that all looked too heavy, too complicated, or too befuddling for Pete to even think about touching.

"I don't know," he said. "This seems kind of hardcore."

"Completely hardcore," William agreed. "But they modify it for beginners. You'll be fine." He waved over the blonde goddess. "Jordanette, this is Pete. He's new, so you'll cut him a few breaks, right?"

Jordanette looked him over, not bothering to hide her skepticism. "We'll scale," she said, and then turned back to a guy with arms like the hulk, both of them covered with bright tattoo sleeves.

"I'm not feeling too welcome."

William shrugged, looking at the instructor's ass as she walked away. "I've tapped that. Pretty sweet."

"My point," Pete said, "is that she doesn't seem too keen on me being here."

"Whatever," William observed. "She is a fitness instructor. She's here to serve you, so don't let her intimidate you. The important thing is that you break yourself in, you get the ball rolling. It is going to feel like shit the first time, but that's cool. It's a first step, right? And you won't believe the results. You in particular."

"Meaning what? I'm out of shape?"

"You are completely out of shape, but that's not what I'm saying. I just meant that, I don't know, it's hard to say. The spirits, man. They like you."

"What do you mean? Things are already tapering off from the lawn business."

"Yeah, that's gonna happen, but you got hit hard, brah. And some of the guys, they didn't get any benefits. Usually it's spread all around, but it looks like you grabbed pretty much the whole pot. That doesn't happen unless they like you."

Pete looked around and saw that some of the guys from the ritual the other night were looking at him, and not in the friendliest way either. It was like – as ridiculous as it sounded – they were jealous of him. These rich, young, fit, handsome guys were jealous of him because the caveman ghosts or whatever had taken a shine to him.

"If they like me already," Pete said, "why do I need to do this?"

William slapped him on the back. "So they'll like you more. You'll see. You've only scratched the surface. You need to make sure you keep getting their attention."

Jordanette blew a whistle, and everyone lined up. Pete got into line next to William, and Jordanette began shouting orders at them like she was a drill sergeant. She made them run and then flip down and do pushups, jumping up after each pushup. They did this an interminable number of times, until Pete thought he was going to vomit, and then they ran some more. Finally, she told them they could stop. The warm-up, she said, was over.

Pete wanted to shout out with rage that this was only the warm-up, but he didn't have the strength. He was bent over, barely breathing, his face hot and his extremities tingling. Meanwhile, everyone else was getting ready for the major workout of the day. They were to do fifty body-weight bench presses, thirty pull-ups, and then twenty body-weight squats. This was to be repeated three times. Everyone lined up to get on the scale to find out what their lifting weight would be.

"I can't do that," Pete complained.

"I told you," Jordanette said, not bothering to hide her impatience. "We'll scale. For you."

Scaling meant that while the other people in the class were bench pressing with multiple massive plates on their bars, Pete was lifting with only one small plate on each end. Then, while they did pull-ups, he used a pull-down machine. Finally, while they squatted massive weights, he did body weight squats, or at least tried to. Jordanette kept yelling at him that his thighs had to be parallel, whatever the hell that meant. It would have been humiliating enough, but when they reached the end, he was more winded than the guys who'd been lifting three times as much as he had.

Pete leaned against the wall, a cone-shaped cup of water in his hand. His heart pounded, his head throbbed. His mouth was so dry it was painful, but drinking didn't help. He felt sure his pulse was erratic, and there was actually a pretty good chance he was going to have a heart attack and die right here.

While he worked on controlling his breathing, William walked over to him and slapped him on the shoulder.

"Fuck," Pete gasped.

"Pretty amaze-balls, right?" William said.

"No," Pete croaked. "It sucked."

"You say that now," he laughed, "but I guarantee you'll be raring to go again when you wake up tomorrow. This is the shit, my man. And let me tell you, you'll see real changes. In your body, sure, but I'm talking about with the other thing. Our helpers, they love it when we live the lifestyle."

Pete waited until after everyone else had finished in the locker room before he showered. In part, he didn't want the guys to see what he looked like under his baggy gym clothes, but the main reason was that if he were to have a heart attack and die, he didn't want it to be while he was naked.

By the time he got back to his car, he was tired and starving and thirsty. Part of him did feel pretty good. There was a certain pleasure in the sensation of his muscles buzzing, his pulse thrumming, all his parts working the way they were supposed to. On the other hand, he figured there would be an even greater pleasure in eating something with a crap load of melted cheese, so he drove to the nearest Taco Cabana and ordered a chicken quesadilla and a margarita and sat by the window, staring at traffic, watching nothing in particular. Mostly he just enjoyed his food and drink and thought about the paleo spirits and how nothing they offered could possibly be as good as Mexican food.

* * *

One chicken quesadilla had been enough, but one margarita proved insufficient, and so he'd ordered a few more. By the time he returned home, his problems had moved from troubling and infuriating to a foggy notion easily dismissed. Things, he decided, were not so bad. He had a wife he loved, and if she were difficult sometimes, so what? That's what marriage was about. Addison was moody and remote, but that was the age. She did well in school, avoided trouble, and seemed to be on the right path. This paleo shit? That didn't matter. He could distance himself from Douchebag William, no problem. It was time to deal with his life his way. He didn't need to follow someone else's rules.

These good feelings lasted about as long as it took him to find Jenny on the couch, a glass of piss-yellow chardonnay in her hand, glaring at him. "I just got off the phone with Rick Hudson," she announced like she was holding up a hammer coated with blood and skull fragments she'd found in his toolbox.

"My condolences," he said, flopping on the couch next to her, letting their legs touch. He was not about to be drawn into a fight.

Jenny shoved herself away from him, a short, quick reflex like a snake lashing out. "He told me you're being sued."

Pete said nothing for a good long time. He stared ahead, trying to figure out how he was going to finesse this, trying to figure out why, exactly, his buzz was gone when only seconds before he'd felt pretty good.

"Well," Jenny demanded.

A rapid succession of thoughts flashed through Pete's mind. He could tell her to mind her own damn business. He could explain that he was the man of the house, that he earned the bread, and that he didn't have to tell her about what went on with his work. Was he supposed to report on every rusty nail that scraped his arm, every time he breathed in a lungful of asbestos? These all seemed like reasonable approaches, but they weren't the way he wanted to go.

"I didn't want to worry you," he said, his voice soft.

"Goddamnit!" she shouted, slamming down her glass. She stood up and began to pace around the room. "Just how fucked are we?"

"I have it under control," he said, knowing that the key here was to believe it, so as to make it believable.

"That's not what Rick says,"

"How the hell does Rick Hudson know, and why is he telling you?"

"A friend of his, a lawyer, mentioned it to him at the health club." *A place you never go,* was implied there, given that she didn't know anything about the ass-kicking he'd taken today at HyperStrong. "He thought maybe, as your wife, I ought to be informed of this sort of thing. This is *my* life we're talking about."

Pete just shook his head. It occurred to him that there was no sympathy here. There was no, *Oh, honey, you can tell me anything.* It was all about her. Jenny wanted to know how Pete's personal and professional ass-fucking was going to affect her ability to buy useless garbage. Pete had tried to do this the nice way, to be all emotional and communicative, but that wasn't getting him anything. Doing what other people wanted him to do was never going to get him anything. Maybe it was time to stop trying.

"Rick says—" Jenny began.

"What do you say we tell Rick to mind his own business?"

"What about my business?" Jenny demanded.

Pete got up and went over to the fridge to grab a beer. "Couldn't tell you," he said. "When you actually have some, you be sure to let me know."

* * *

Pete stayed up drinking hours after Jenny stomped to the bedroom and turned out the light. Each can he put back felt like an act of defiance, against Jenny, against William, against sneering Jordanette, and against the caveman spirits. While he was at it, he was defying Candi Watson and Rick Hudson as well, though how was not quite clear to him. Not that it mattered. Fuck them. When he finally went to bed, it was with the feeling that he had no idea what could happen next.

It turned out to be a ghost dog. That's what could happen next.

It jumped on him in the middle of the night and, contrary to what Pete would have expected from ghost dog teeth, tried to tear his throat out.

He awoke with the sudden feeling of a weight landing on his chest, and then the head of breath bearing down on him. He knew it was their dead dog, Howard, though he couldn't have said how. It was just something he understood – that it had returned, and it was angry. There were slashes, painful tears, as claws scrambled for purchase, tearing through his pajama top. In the ambient light of the bedroom, Pete could see there was nothing there, but he could feel it and he could smell it, and he knew exactly what it was.

Pete put out his hands defensively as this *thing*, this mass of pressure and will and anger, moved toward him. Sharp teeth grazed at the skin of his throat. The stench of rot and sour breath filled his nostrils. This thing he couldn't see was moving in to kill him. He knew he must have looked ridiculous, lying in bed, flailing around next to his impossibly still-sleeping wife, but he didn't care. He didn't want her to wake up and find him, his throat torn out, lying dead next to her. The thing strained toward him, its teeth moving in for the kill, and in a sudden burst of power from his HyperStrong-sore muscles, Pete managed to toss the animal off him, to his left, which happened to be Jenny's side of the bed.

In spite of Pete's struggles and his grunts, Jenny had still not stirred, but the dog's ghost nails raked her cheek as it flew, cutting three big gashes in her flesh. Jenny awoke with a start, sitting up, shouting.

"What's going on?" she demanded, putting her hand to her cheek. She switched on the light, glaring at him, the jagged lines across her left cheek just beginning to bloom.

Pete, who knew he must look crazed, with his hair wild, his pajamas askew, said nothing at first. He listened, waiting to hear the ghost dog, to figure out what angle it would choose for its next attack, but nothing came. Jenny started to speak again, but he shushed her, holding up a hand.

There was nothing. Just the distant hum of the air conditioner and his own panting breath. Howard had gone.

"What the hell are you doing?" Jenny demanded.

Pete opened his mouth, but he knew the ghost dog story was not going to carry a whole lot of weight. Instead he shook his head and gasped for air like a freshly caught fish.

"I had a dream," he finally managed.

"A dream?" She pressed a finger to her cheek and looked at the glistening drops of blood that jiggled on the tip. "A dream?"

"That's what I said," he told her calmly, like she was the crazy one, like his own clothes weren't torn and he didn't have bloody scratches covering his chest. "I'm sorry I got you."

"No you're not," she insisted. "This is – what? Payback?"

He reached out for her. "Jenny…"

She backed out of bed, like he was some kind of a sicko, like he'd scratched her in her sleep to be cruel. "Don't touch me," she hissed. "This is… this is abuse."

"It was an accident," Pete said, feeling himself get angry that he had to lie about it. It wasn't even as much his fault as if it had been an accident, and she ought to believe him. What, in all their years together, would make her believe he would deliberately, in the dead of night, scratch her cheek? It should be obvious to her that he wouldn't hurt her, and if he were going to, is this really how he would go about it? "Let me help you clean up."

"Fuck you," she said. "I'm calling the police. And this much I promise you. This is the last time you'll ever do this to me. And don't expect to be let near Addison ever again."

"What?" Pete cried. "I'd never hurt Addison."

"But you'd hurt me?"

Pete felt overwhelmed by her logic. He couldn't find words.

"Don't worry, Pete," she said, mustering all the bitterness at her disposal, which was not an inconsiderable amount. "You won't have the chance. I'll make sure you never see either of us except through metal bars."

He watched, helpless, as she picked up the phone. There was blood on his own fingers, he didn't know if it was hers or the dog's, and he stared at it dumfounded as Jenny pushed three buttons on the phone.

A strange kind of clarity overtook him. This was real, here and now, and she was actually doing it. She was calling 911, and they were going to arrest him. He was going to be fingerprinted and put in the county jail, and he would have to get a lawyer. There would be more financial ruin, and his life, as he knew it, would be over. No matter how things shook out, no matter if the charges were dropped, he would still be the guy who attacked his wife. His marriage was done. Could Jenny really keep him from seeing his daughter? Even if she couldn't, his relationship with Addison would never be the same again. Her revulsion toward him wouldn't be simply ordinary adolescent hormonal irritation. She would think her father was a creep and a psycho, someone to shun. Pete was watching everything he cared about unravel.

He didn't know why he did it – some weird instinct, a memory of something powerful and effective – but while she held the phone he quickly moved his finger on the headboard, making the same symbols William had made on the stone altar. Using his own blood he made the three spiraling circles, and in their center, a handprint. Even as he was doing it, he felt like he was being foolish, giving Jenny more ammunition to claim he was insane. *He was painting in his own blood!* But it also felt like taking care of business, like doing what had to get done, so he finished the task.

"Nine-one-one," he heard over the line. "What's your emergency?"

"I'm sorry," Jenny said. "I made a mistake."

She hung up the phone as if in a dream. She sat there, her hands in her lap, looking at Pete, and suddenly not angry. She looked – he didn't quite know – like she was waiting for something. Orders, maybe? It was worth a shot.

"Can I help you clean up that scratch?" he asked her.

"Please," she said.

He took her hand and led her to the bathroom. With a washcloth dipped in warm water, he gently dabbed at the scratches. He had deliberately chosen white washcloths to see if she'd complain about staining them, but Jenny said nothing. When he was finished, Jenny stood over the sink, impassive, while pink water swirled down the drain, and then remained still while Pete dabbed on some antibiotic cream. The scratches were broad, but not deep, and they would be healed in a few days.

They both changed into fresh night clothes. They straightened out the bed clothes, making the scene of the crime look neat, like nothing had happened. Jenny fell asleep crying, letting Pete hold her.

* * *

The next morning, the magic caveman symbol was hard to discern on the wooden headboard, but the power still seemed to be in effect. Jenny walked around in a daze, getting breakfast for her family, making small talk, smiling, but seeming to be distracted. She had loaded a ton of makeup on top of her wounds, and they were all but invisible unless you knew what to look for.

Pete was glad she wasn't angry with him anymore, but she was also not terribly communicative. He didn't mind the end of hostilities, but Pete didn't want a robot wife. He wanted the old Jenny back, and if he had to keep making caveman symbols in blood to do that, it was a price he was willing to pay, but all the paleo magic in the world couldn't make her into something she wasn't. Pete had the feeling the Jenny from the previous night –

angry, resentful, nasty – was still in there, trapped beneath this creepy compliance, pounding on the invisible glass of her consciousness. He had turned his wife into a prisoner in her own body.

He felt like crap about robbing his wife of her free will, of making her, against her nature, a servant to his whims, but he'd deal with that later. Best to take things one step at a time.

Addison got off to school, and Jenny went off to the bedroom to sit quietly and stare into space. Her face had begun to twitch, like the power of the symbol was wearing off, so Pete figured it was time to get the hell out of there before she realized he had used some sort of evil trick to help her clean her wounds. Then the yelling would begin again. Pete got into his truck and made it as far as the end of the driveway when he stopped.

Something didn't sit right with him about the argument from the previous night. It made no sense that Rick Hudson would call Jenny to tell her about the lawsuit. What would make him assume she didn't already know? Pete turned off the car and took out his phone to call his private detective friend, Grant.

Checking up on your wife, Grant assured him, is pretty much always a bad idea. There was almost never anything good that came of this sort of thing. Pete, however, didn't want to live in ignorance. He put in the order. He then told Grant about the other business he wanted looked into.

"That's a lot of leg work," Grant said. "I can give you a cut rate, but I still have to pay labor."

"It doesn't matter," Pete told him. "You've got to spend money to make money."

"More people should have that attitude about their marriages," Grant said.

Just as he ended the call, here was Douchebag William coming out of his house and walking toward his car. Pete got out of his truck and ran over to him.

"Hey," he said. "The spirit of my dead dog attacked me last night."

"Huh," William said. "That's weird."

"Weird," Pete said. "Jesus Christ, man, what the hell is going on?"

"That's just how this shit works sometimes," William said with a *wait-until-next-season* shrug. "You ever open a door for some hottie and a fat chick also comes through, like you were holding the door for her all along? That's what happened. You opened a door, brah. You can't keep things from walking in and out. The only way to stay on top of the situation is to live right, like the cavemen did. Stay away from carbs. Work out hard. That's the key."

"So, my dead dog attacked me because I ate a quesadilla?" Pete said.

William shrugged. "None of us are experts in this. We don't know exactly how it works, but we know what we've had success with. Living like cavemen is what keeps us powerful, and what keeps these spirits or powers or whatever it is in line."

"Living like cavemen didn't really help the cavemen, did it? They're all gone."

"You're thinking too narrowly, man. You've been straining against the way. I get that. Old habits are hard to break. But you're in this now, and you have to stick with it, or this is going to completely fuck up your life."

"What do you mean?" Pete said, though he was beginning to suspect he already knew.

"Like I told you, man. Open doors. And the thing about some doors is they're easier to open than they are to close. You're going to have dead dogs or psychopathic shamans or vengeful car spirits or whatever up your ass 24/7 if you don't get your shit in line. You think you're being all badass and defiant by drinking beer and eating carbs, but you're not fucking with *me*, Pete. You are fucking with cosmic forces. You either make those powers do your bidding, or they'll make you their bitch."

Pete stood on the driveway, blinking against the still-rising sun, trying to process all of this new information. And that was the thing. It was new. "Why didn't you tell me all this before we started?"

William shrugged. "I guess I forgot."

* * *

Pete managed to make it through the rest of the day, but it was all nagging at him. Was Jenny having an affair – with Rick Hudson of all people? Was he really stuck dealing with beerlessness and dead dogs for the rest of his life because William forgot to tell him about the caveman pact?

He was driving home, deciding he needed one of those beers he was supposed to be avoiding, when he passed a bar he'd always been curious about. It was a smoky, windowless concrete block on one of the major streets he passed regularly. He'd gone by it a million times but had never gone inside. What the hell, Pete thought. He didn't want to go home, and if you're going to drink alone at a bar, it might as well be one where no one knows you.

Not surprisingly, there weren't a whole lot of people inside. It was still just four in the afternoon. There was a table where three guys in their forties sat talking in hushed tones, and there was a Mexican guy, in his thirties and fat as shit, sitting at the bar. Pete took a seat at the bar about as far from the fat Mexican as he could manage and ordered a Coors from a balding bartender with white hair who looked like he'd passed retirement age a few decades back. Then, because why the hell not, he ordered a shot of Jack. Then he repeated the whole thing a few times because his life now included the kind of shit that made you want to drink.

After a while, he began to wonder if there was maybe something wrong with this place. A few more people had come in, and they were all looking at him like he was some kind of an asshole, which he had given them no reason to suspect. Then he noticed the fat Mexican guy kept glancing over at him. Somehow he'd moved a few stools closer. The guy was still looking after the bartender set down Pete's fourth beer and whiskey combo. That was about as much as a guy could reasonably be expected to take. Pete turned his neck and met the guy's brown eyes square on.

"Help you with something?"

The guy got up and sat next to Pete. "I'm Mike," he said with a kind of sideways grin.

"Yeah?" Pete answered, taking an aloof drink of his beer. "Is that a fact?"

"Hey, I'm just being friendly, man," Mike said, showing his puffy hands. "No need get all hostile."

"Go be friendly somewhere else," Pete said. "I'm not here to talk." That wasn't necessarily true. When Pete had first thought of heading into a bar, he'd imagined himself making friends, laughing, eating pretzels, and watching a game on TV, but it had turned out to be a solitary experience, and he was settling into that. He didn't really want it disturbed. Besides, something about this guy and his big eyes and his soft spoken manner rubbed him the wrong way.

"You have a rough day?" Mike asked.

Pete shook his head. He didn't know where to begin, but he knew he didn't want to even make the effort with this guy.

"Sometimes it helps to let off a little steam," Mike proposed.

"I told you, I'm not here to talk," Pete told him.

Mike grinned. "We don't have to talk if you don't want. We can go out to my van."

Pete felt his shoulder pulling back so he could punch the guy, but then he suddenly realized what was off about the place. No windows. Just men. This was a gay bar. He was in a gay bar. Him. Pete. He was being propositioned by a guy who thought a dick in the ass was the sort of thing you should be cheerful about. The guy wanted to go out to his van so they could do what? Have some kind of butt sex? Give each other blow jobs? Fondle one another's testicles?

Pete suddenly realized he was rock hard. A dizzying confusion washed over him because he knew in his heart that he was absolutely not gay. And even if he were – and this was just entertaining the possibility for the purposes of making a point – he was pretty sure he would not want to mess around with fat Mike. He'd been at a casting call for the Chippendale boys the day before, and he'd never had a single gay thought, so he knew that wasn't the issue.

He just needed to fuck.

"Your cocked fist says no," Mike observed with a grin, looking down at Pete's pants, "but your cock says yes."

He punched Mike in the face because he also needed to hit someone. It wasn't because he hated queers. That would have been an overstatement. He didn't really like them, but he didn't like most people, so really, when you thought about it, Pete treated gays like he treated everyone else. Isn't that what equality was all about?

Fat Mike was on the floor, limbs waving around like an upturned cockroach. The other guys were now getting up, moving closer to him. The geezer behind the bar was now holding an aluminum baseball bat. The odds were against him, but Pete didn't care. In fact, he kind of liked the feeling of just how fucked he was because he knew he was getting out of this. He'd fought off a dead dog last night. A bar fight with a bunch of cupcakes was going to be no problem.

* * *

On the way home, he was pulled over by an Alamo Heights police car. He'd been driving erratically in part because he'd put down a shitload of booze in less than an hour, and also because the bar fight with a bunch of cupcakes had been more of a problem than anticipated. He'd held his own, and the aluminum baseball bat had never come into play, which was certainly in the plus column. Besides, it had felt great. Taking and throwing punches. It had turned out to be some kind of crazy Fight Club action, and when two of the guys grabbed his arms and Mike had slammed him in the gut, Pete had been thinking that maybe this was what he'd been missing in his life. Maybe all these years of saying *Yes, dear* to Jenny and saying *Yes, sir* to rich people who wanted to buy gigantic houses had taken something away from him.

The solution, he'd realized almost at once, was not getting smacked around by gay people. Neither was it flipping monster-truck tires and swearing off beer. Pete needed to stop doing what everyone else wanted him to do. Jenny wanted him to keep in line and let her act like they made twice as much money as they did. William was telling him he had to live his life like Piltdown Man. Mike wanted him to ride the sodomy train to Buttfuck Station. Fuck all of them.

He'd made it out of there, getting in a few more blows, taking a couple of big hits – one of the ear, which was still ringing, and one to the nose, which was definitely not broken, but was bleeding enthusiastically. The bottom line, as the flashing lights danced over him, was that shitfaced and bloody was not the best way to present yourself when a policeman pulled you over.

Pete sat there, drunk out of his mind, his knuckles bleeding from the fight, considering himself basically fucked. The cop sat in the car interminably, doing whatever it was they did before actually hauling their asses out. Then his door opened, the guy sauntered over, like he was hot shit. Pete watched him from the rearview mirror and thought that he recognized the baby-faced guy from somewhere. Then it came to him. It was the same cop who had kicked him out of the Candi Watson's real estate office. The only bright spot in all of this was that while seeing this jerkoff again was a humiliation for Pete, there was no way the cop would remember him.

"Remember me?" the cop asked before requesting Pete's documentation.

"You get that redhead with the big tits to go out with you?" Pete asked him.

The cop didn't say anything. He didn't grin. He didn't say she was too fat or whatever. There was no cracking the ice of his professional demeanor.

The cop took Pete's driver's license and disappeared for a good long while, checking on things that required absolutely no checking. Then he came back and leaned against the window. "Sir, are you aware that you are bleeding?"

"I got into a fight with a bunch of homosexuals," Pete said. "As an American, I believe they have the same right to get their asses kicked as anyone else."

"Sir, have you been drinking tonight?"

"I had a few," Pete said. "Within the legal limit."

"Sir, I am going to have to ask you to step out of the vehicle."

"Have you ever noticed," Pete inquired, "that you have a habit of telling people what you are about to say? Why not just say it?"

"Sir," the cop said, "get out of the vehicle."

Pete really did not want to do this. He was both legally and legitimately drunk, and giving drunks a pass did not seem to be on the cop's agenda. For the second time in less than 24 hours, Pete was facing the ruin through arrest. This sort of thing had never happened before. Now it was twice daily? Sooner or later, he was going to hit the end of the road. Maybe this was the exact moment his life would head down the shitter. People like to look back and wonder where it all went wrong. Pete didn't have to wonder. He didn't have to reflect later. This was it, here and now.

He didn't even decide to do it. It just happened. He wiped his hand against the slow drip of blood from his nose. Then he reached forward to the dashboard and began to trace the three swirls. It was a few quick motions. It was a risk, of course. The cop might somehow misinterpret the gesture as hostile, but he had to take the risk. In a few quick gestures he hacked out the symbols and placed his palm print in the center. Then he got out of the car.

The cop stood there, staring at him for a long while, like trying to remember who Pete was and why they both were there. Then he handed Pete his license. "Have a good night, sir."

The cop got in his car and drove away, and Pete went back into his car and sat, holding his license as he came to the understanding that he was not fucked at all. He was not fucked in the least. He was un-fucked. This weird symbol was his get out of jail free card – pretty much literally. How did Douchebag William not know this? Had he never tried it? Did it not work for him? Pete had no idea, and, frankly, he didn't give a shit. All he knew was that he didn't have to live by anyone else's rules. This was not the moment his life fell apart. It was the moment it all came together.

* * *

Despite this decision, Pete's routine did not change much over the next few days. Then, all at once, two events more or less changed him forever.

The first was a call from Grant, who wanted Pete to stop by his office. Pete knew what Grant was going to say, and he wished he could turn back the clock, choose not to have Grant inquire into Jenny. That would have been smarter, but it was too late for that now. There was no putting the genie back in the bottle. So he sat there, in Grant's dingy office, pictures of sports cars on the wall, while his old high school buddy slid a folder over to him.

Grant looked like a mirror image of Pete. They were both losing their hair, both overweight. They had gotten into a lot of trouble back in high school, broken a lot of rules, raised a lot of hell, but now here they were, middle aged, shadows of what they had hoped to be.

"It's not too late," Grant said. "You don't have to open it."

"I kind of do," Pete said.

Grant nodded. "Yeah, telling people that is bullshit, but I say it because it makes me sound wise and full of insight. Like I'm Yoda or something."

The pictures were blurry, taken on the fly, but quality wasn't the point. Jenny and Rick Hudson, holding hands, kissing, slipping into the casita in the back of his house.

Pete sat still for a long time. He looked at the photos, and then replaced them back in the folder. He didn't say much of anything. Grant didn't say anything either. Pete figured he had experience with these kinds of situations, and he knew how to handle them.

Finally Grant handed over another envelope. "This is the other thing you wanted. I think it's better news. I don't imagine it makes you feel much better right now."

Pete shrugged. "I don't really know what I feel," he said, and it was true enough.

"You want to get a couple of hookers?" Grant asked. "I make a lot of contacts in this job."

"Maybe later," Pete said. He needed time to think.

* * *

He was still in a daze when he pulled up into his driveway. William had been across the street, sitting on his stoop, looking at his phone. He'd obviously been waiting for Pete. Now he came running over.

"I need to talk to you, brah."

"This isn't a great time," Pete said.

"Yeah, well, it's not a great time for me either. We had a gathering last night—"

Pete looked up sharply. After what he'd just learned about Jenny, this still stung him. He'd been invited to join their little caveman group, and now they were having meetings without him. "A gathering, huh?"

"Look, don't be insulted. You've just been, you know, impure. We didn't want that contaminating our shit. The point is that we were getting nothing. I kind of feel like, I don't know, the powers have attached themselves to you. Like you're hoarding it all for yourself."

As soon as William said it, Pete knew it was true. He hadn't exactly been hoarding. That suggested he had done it on purpose, but he knew the basic truth of what William was saying. The caveman spirits were his.

"And you want them back?" Pete asked.

"That's right."

"No problem." Pete reached into his back pocket. "Oh, wait. I forgot. Fuck you."

William put on his best reasonable lawyer face. "Come on, man. No need to be that way."

"What way is that? You lied to me. You led me into this shit without telling me what was going on, and now I'm going to do things my way."

"I don't think that's such a good idea. You don't want to cross us."

"Yeah, what's going to happen if I do?"

William stood still for a moment, as if considering his options, thinking about which method was going to win the day. Then, without warning, he took a swing. It was a wild roundhouse, right at Pete's head, but Pete saw it coming a mile away. He ducked, and then jabbed up hard, smacking William under the jaw. His already bruised knuckles stung like a motherfucker, but he didn't care. He took too much pleasure in the sight of William staggering backwards.

William paused, pressed a couple of probing fingers to his jaw, spit out a glob of blood. "What the fuck, man?" he shouted, like Pete's violence had been inexplicable. Then he lunged at Pete again.

For Pete, the world seemed to have slowed while his senses heightened. It was like in a movie. He wanted to shout something out, just for the pleasure of hearing his words come out all low and distended. He was too busy kicking William's ass, however. Another swing came, and Pete deftly stepped aside, and with William over-extended, Pete slammed him in the gut. William staggered, and for good measure, Pete kneed him in the nuts.

William dropped to the ground, moaning, his hands covering his wounded package.

"The world has been kicking me in the nuts all my life," Pete said. "Now you know how it feels."

William did not seem to appreciate the deftness of Pete's metaphor. He was too busy gasping for air, rolling on the grass with his hands tucked between his legs, and looking like he might vomit. That was when the reality of the situation began to wash over Pete. He had kicked William's ass. He had just beat the crap out of a guy who had the size and strength and skill to completely crush Pete. More than that, he'd done it because he had these caveman spirits on his side. He hadn't won them over by giving up things he liked or doing a bunch of bullshit that made him miserable. He did it by being himself. It was like all that stupid self-esteem garbage they dumped on Addison when she was in school – Be yourself! You are wonderful! Celebrate you! – only this was so much better because it involved eating quesadillas and drinking beer.

"They don't want us to be like them," Pete said, the truth of it coming into focus. "They want us to be what we are. You're so busy chasing the latest fad, trying to figure out what you should be doing, that you don't know what you *want* to be doing. I know what I want. That's what they respect."

Or maybe it was something else. Maybe it was a total fluke that they were helping him. Maybe it was his hair color or his shoe size. How the fuck should Pete know? But it sounded good, and, more importantly, it made him sound like he knew what he was talking about.

"Now, get off my property."

* * *

Jenny was waiting for him inside the house, standing in an awkward position, holding a dishrag as if she had teleported from the kitchen. "What the hell was that? Fighting on the lawn?"

Pete was slightly stooped over. His breath was coming in rapid bursts, and his clothes were a mess. His knuckles were raw and throbbing, and there was blood all over his hand. Nevertheless, he felt fantastic, and he grinned while he bent over double and caught his breath. "You saw?"

"Yes, I saw," Jenny said, clutching the towel like she was trying to strangle it. "It was disgusting."

Pete stood up and walked over to the fridge for a beer. How come, he wondered, there was always plenty of beer there? They ran out of juice and milk and soda all the time, but Jenny never forgot to replace the brews. Was this her way of keeping him contained, locked away in a cage of drunken cluelessness? That had backfired, he thought as the tab came back like a gunshot.

"That guy should have owned me," Pete said, taking a sip. "Why didn't you come out? You didn't think I needed help?"

"What should I have done? Hit him in the head with a frying pan?"

Pete smiled at the thought of that. "That would have been something."

"I don't believe you. Can't you see how far you're letting yourself fall."

"You don't get it," he said. "I'm not falling. I'm on my way up. I should be teaching other guys about this like a self-help guru or something. I've got wisdom now." He knew it was true. Everything was about to change for him. He could feel it, and, in spite of what she'd done, he wanted Jenny around for the next phase of his life. He was willing to forgive her – mostly. This thing, with the caveman spirits or whatever they were, was an opportunity to completely remake their lives.

It occurred to him that she had no idea he knew about Rick Hudson. If he didn't know about her cheating, then he could move beyond it without humiliating himself. He didn't have to give ground here. He could have things back the way they used to be, only better.

Pete stepped forward and took her hand. "I know we've had a rough patch lately, but maybe we can put it all behind us. Maybe we can start over again. Things can be like they used to be. They can be better."

Jenny pulled her hand away. Her face wrinkled up like he was a *thing*, like he was violating her by even trying to make contact. "You're disgusting."

He watched her walk away, disappear into the hallway. He was still standing there when the bedroom door slammed. No blow William could have delivered would have hurt like this. His own wife thought he was vile, filthy, not fit to be touched.

Not everything was going to go his way. He had to understand that. He'd just have to make the best of what he had, and if people didn't like that, then maybe they shouldn't have fucked with him in the first place. That was the sort of thing he would say when he went on the lecture circuit.

* * *

Pete had no idea how this stuff worked. He was flying by the seat of his pants here, but he figured his instincts had gotten him this far, he might as well keep on trusting them. The next day, after Jenny and Addison were out of the house, he returned home. He heated up a frozen pizza, one loaded with meat and extra cheese. Once it was cooked, he ate it while drinking a six pack. He cut his finger, and drew the swirling, caveman symbol onto an undershirt, drinking the last of the six while it dried.

This, he figured, would protect him. With the shirt on under his button down, he got into his truck and drove over to Candi's office.

This time, the plump redhead sent him right in. Candi was sitting behind her desk, looking perfectly composed in her expensive white blouse, open one button too many. Her lipstick was freshly applied and glistening. For a woman in her sixties, Pete decided, she wasn't half bad. A little brittle, maybe, but still kind of sexy. In fact, he thought he knew how this had to go in order to appease the caveman spirits.

Pete closed the door behind him.

Candi held up a hand, but she looked amused, not angry. "Pete, I know what you're going to say."

Pete threw himself into the chair across from her. "That you fucked me over?"

"It was just business," she said, lilting her words to bring out the Texas, like what she'd done was all charming and sweet when you looked at it from the right angle.

Pete threw a manila envelope onto her desk. It was the one Grant had given him in his office.

"It occurred to me," Pete said, "that maybe I wasn't the first person you tried this with. Maybe I'm the first one to get screwed over, but I figure if you slipped me a little money to tweak the system, you'd tried it before. It was just a sale, after all. You weren't desperate. It was business as usual. So, I asked my private investigator buddy to do a little digging. I asked him to check out the other inspectors you deal with, and once he got them in a room with a lawyer, three of them were willing to admit they'd taken bribes from you. Now, that's all off the record, but if my legal problem doesn't go away, then I'm going to sue you, and then what those guys have to say will be on the record. I don't even have to win, because everyone in town will know you've paid inspectors to bury information from your clients. And that means you'll be finished, and if you think I have legal problems now, I can promise you that's nothing. The rich assholes will be lining up to take your money."

Candi remained motionless for a moment, and then her mouth twitched just a little. "So, what do you want, Pete?"

"I want you to take care of the client and their roof, like you promised you would," he said. "I don't care how. Pay for the repairs out of your own pocket. You won't even miss money like that. And then you need to change your tune about me. Talk me up. Send business my way. All I want is for things to be like they were before you took a complete dump on my life."

"And if I do that, what do you do with this?" she gestured toward the envelope on her desk.

Pete shrugged. "I don't want a war with you, Candi. That never goes anywhere so long as you hold up your end of the bargain. Oh, and pay the private detective's bill. Grant's my friend and all, but digging up your dirt was expensive."

"I can do that," she said. Just like that. She was doing what he wanted. She leaned forward, letting the top of her blouse hang open. "And what else can I do for you?"

* * *

There were a bunch of reasons why Pete decided to go ahead and have sex with Candi Watson in her office. The idea of putting it to a woman who had treated him like dirt for so long was too sweet to resist. The six pack he'd put down while making his t-shirt was still swimming through his system, and that probably played a role in it too. Most of all he did it because it felt like what he was supposed to be doing, and as near as he could tell, that's what drove the system. That's what made things go his way. Having sex with a near-retirement-age realtor was the ritual the spirits demanded of him, so he did it.

There was also the fact that if Jenny could step out on him, he could do the same, but he wasn't sure he wanted to brag about this one.

* * *

Next up was Rick's place. Grant said they'd been using his casita out back as their rendezvous place, and he'd said lunch hour was the time, so Rick drove over, parking his car a couple of blocks away. He just walked around back, through the fence, and opened the door.

In the movies, the cheating couple is always caught in the act, but really, what are the odds? There's a lot more time spent in before and after, and it turned out that Pete got the after. Jenny and Rick were both in the process of dressing when Pete walked into the casita. They froze. Rick in his t-shirt and boxers, one leg going into his suit pants. Jenny had her back to the door, but was turning, her mouth a little O of surprise as she latched her bra.

Pete didn't want for there to be a whole lot of conversation. There wasn't much to say. He smacked Rick in the face, a big open-palm slap that, given his awkward pose, sent him sprawling to the carpet. Jenny screamed.

No one was telling him it was not what it looked like, which was good. Pete didn't want to mess around with that bullshit.

"Look at you," Jenny said, her face having moved from surprise to anger. "You come here stinking of beer and you slap him, like you fought with our neighbor. Is that what you are now? A drunken brawler?"

Pete felt himself nodding. "I guess it is. I don't think it's all of what I am, but that's part of it, sure."

"Get out!" Jenny screamed.

"I'm not quite ready to get out."

Rick was now on his feet. He'd managed to get his pants on, which was better for his dignity. "Now, look, Pete. I know this is uncomfortable, we shouldn't deal with this when tempers are running hot. Why don't we go somewhere and talk about it like civilized people."

"Somewhere your wife won't find out about?" Pete asked.

"There's no need for this thing to blow up in our faces, is there?" Rick smiled at him. "I know you've been having some hard times, so what's it going to take to make this right?"

Pete stared at him. He'd been pushing back against the worst of his impulses. He wanted violence. He wanted to inflict pain and take in the coppery smell of blood, but he'd been holding himself back. He kept telling himself that it didn't have to be that way, but maybe it should be that way. "Rick, did you just try to bribe me into letting you have my wife?"

"She's not yours anymore. I'm just trying to take the sting out of it."

Pete hit him in the face. Rick staggered back, bounced off the wall, and came at Pete, arms waving wildly. Pete hit him again. And again. Rick's nose burst open, spraying blood in a fine mist. Pete tasted Rick's nose blood on his mouth. He licked his lips. There was blood in the air, and the powers were satisfied.

"Leave him alone!"

Pete turned in time to see his wife rushing at him with a cheese knife. Why was there a cheese knife in the casita? It was a good question, but Pete didn't have a chance to ponder it. Jenny's eyes were wild, her muscles tensed. Pete could see it all. Her rage, her angle, the shoes she'd left on the floor. He merely stepped out of the way, let Jenny slip, let her fall forward, cheese knife in hand. He watched as it made contact with Rick's throat, and he saw the explosive mist of arterial blood as it streaked across his wife's face.

A shudder passed through Pete, revulsion and regret and relief. The powers had their blood, and they would be satisfied for now.

Pete glanced around the room, dazed, heart pumping, mind racing. There was a platter with cheese and crackers on the dresser. That explained the knife.

* * *

The last few months had been hard on Addison to be sure. With her mother arrested for killing her lover, and all the local media attention the case had produced, a change of scenery was just the thing. Pete stood on the lawn and watched the movers load up the truck. Across the street, William's old house stood empty. The Douche had moved out a couple of weeks before, but he hadn't been able to find a buyer. Pete had considered snatching up the place himself, but there were too many weird memories.

Now that his web business was taking off – Pete had one of those sites where people paid money for a downloaded book, his on how to achieve your goals by indulging in what makes you happy – the world was opening up before him. There had been some setbacks, sure. Jenny's legal fees, for one. Pete had considered throwing her to the wolves. No one would have blamed him after how she'd treated him, sure, but that would have sent the wrong message to Addison. Instead he hired a relatively inexpensive lawyer.

Rick's death was, of course, a colossal mess, but no one was going for first degree murder charges. Pete told the police it was an accident. In his version, he'd caught the two of them having an affair, Rick had attacked Pete, and when Pete fought back, Jenny came at her husband with the knife. She hadn't meant to kill Rick, he'd said. It was an accident. The plea deal gave her a chance of getting out in ten years.

"Things are going to be better," he told Addison. "You'll see." Pete leaned over and kissed the top of her head. She gave him a hug back. That was one positive aspect to all of this. Addison had dropped the attitude. She'd realized just how much she needed her dad, and he was there for her. He'd have to be a bad person not to be.

Pete smiled at her again. A new town. A new start. He could have whatever he wanted, and if things got a little messy along the way, that was just life.

The End

David Liss is the author of nine novels, most recently *The Day of Atonement* and *Randoms,* his first book for younger readers. His previous bestselling books include *The Coffee Trader* and *The Ethical Assassin*, both of which are being developed as films, and ***A Conspiracy of Paper,*** which is now being developed for television. Liss is the author of numerous comics, including *Mystery Men, Sherlock Holmes*: *Moriarty Lives* and *Angelica Tomorrow*

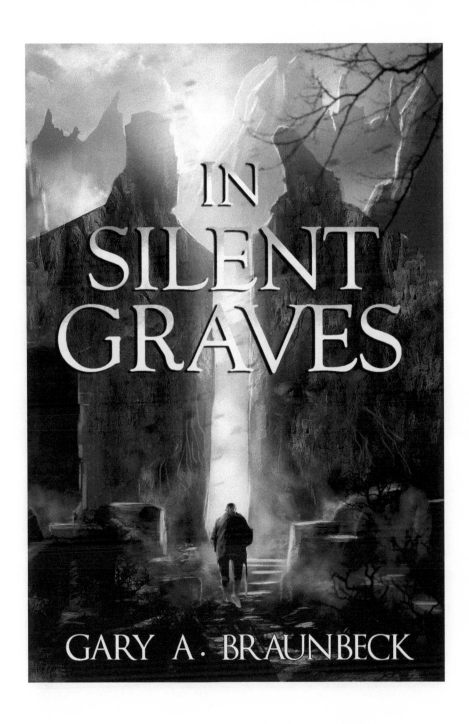

IN
SILENT
GRAVES

GARY A · BRAUNBECK

SOUL MATES

JOHN R. LITTLE

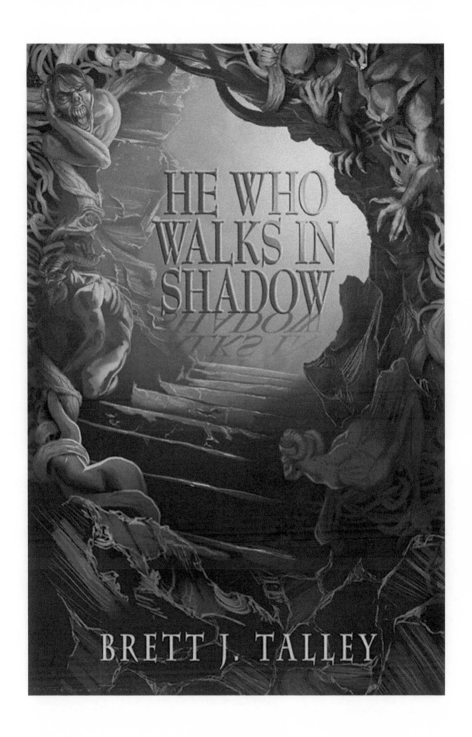

HE WHO
WALKS IN
SHADOW

BRETT J. TALLEY

DIVINE
SCREAM

A NOVEL

BENJAMIN KANE ETHRIDGE
BRAM STOKER AWARD® WINNING AUTHOR